Post-Regina
Chronicles of the Floating City
& the Night Carnival
Book 3

A Found Letter. From the Archives and Commentaries of the Stewards [Artifact Not Numbered, Thought to be Dated 40 years Post Regina]

Archival Notation
I cannot verify the source of this letter. There is no Miriam that I can find. There was once a Mae in the Menagerie District, a clockmaker, but there is no further record of her or any surviving relations. If this is true, it is unbelievable. I dare not share this with the others. We have just started to recover. This artifact will remain unnumbered, uncategorized, hidden in plain sight. I will read it into the record.

Miriam,

This letter will never reach you. It is by unimaginable risk that I write it, and sending it is inconceivable. I will not speak these things aloud, but I must address them to somebody. It is you, Miriam. Always to you.

Miriam, maybe I betrayed my city. Maybe I should have said something when Jackdaw, the clockwork bird, began to go missing. Maybe with my silence, I have plunged us into further mayhem. But I wanted to see what he would do. The clockworks only go where assigned, but Jackdaw, he left the menagerie on his own, night after night. I found him playing chess. Yes, Miriam, chess, every week in Foundry Alley, with the crucible maker. It looked like the same game, even. A chess game that did not end. A year, this continued, and I said nothing. Miriam, they are still playing this chess game.

Miriam, Jackdaw brought a necklace to the Queen the night before her execution. I know this because a whole to-do was made of this necklace showing up. It was assumed to be a gift from the people, maybe a parting gift, before they lopped her head off. Jackdaw was the only clockwork unaccounted for when they say the necklace arrived, and how else could it have gotten there? No one has claimed responsibility for sending it, and these people, they are vicious. Someone would have bragged. I saw the necklace, Miriam, and it was made with a fine alloy ribbon that fit the Queen's throat perfectly. I would have recognized that ribbon anywhere. It is the sort we make. But there was something else about it.

On the day of the execution, when the Queen walked to the chopping block with Coyote at her side, the necklace seemed to shift and move, like a snake. Like a snake, Miriam, I swear on The Nameless.

Miram, the execution was a disaster. The heralds in the streets call it a triumph, they claim the people called to see the Queen hanged and not beheaded at the last minute, but Miriam, it's because the clockwork we built especially for this execution went missing. We still cannot find it anywhere. It was a gorgeous beast, Miram, as tall as two and a half men, with a human-like body and the head of a bull. When we were unable to provide a proper executioner, no one was willing to cut off the Queen's head. With the Bone People gone, no one would get close enough to her to do it. I swear, Miriam, the little Queen could have just walked off that platform and left, and no one would have stopped Her. Everyone was afraid to touch Her. We had to do something, Miriam. We promised the citizens an execution. So we told Coyote to hang Her. So, Coyote led Her to the Temple of Condition and we hung Her there in the courtyard, and we rang the giant bell, and the people celebrated their victory.

We intended to leave Her there for a few days, for the people to look upon and be inspired.

In the morning, Her body was gone. We told the people the devils had claimed Her.

But Miriam, I saw what happened.

I saw Coyote cut Her down from the belfry and carry Her away. I saw Jackdaw release the clasp of the necklace, and Miriam, Nameless forgive me, Miriam, I saw the Queen gasp for air and wretch in Coyote's arms. I do not know where they have taken Her or what they plan to do with Her. This is madness, Miriam, I am speaking of clockworks having plans.

In the morning Coyote and Jackdaw were back in the menagerie as usual. Nothing is amiss. The people have instituted a new festival, a celebration of the first bell. The Festival of Bells, they say, to commemorate their freedom. But Miriam, the Queen is not dead. If I tell anyone what I know, they will hang me. They will not believe the clockworks acted without instruction. They will think it is a conspiracy among the machinists. Miriam, I am an old woman, I want to live my days out peacefully, as peacefully as I can, after these years of war.

Sister, I am afraid. What sorceries we have used to build these clockworks, have the clockworks learned, themselves?

I want to say I hope this letter finds you well, but I know it will not find you. All I want for the both of us, is something warm. A soft bed. A full night's sleep. A week without burning buildings. I want the ash in the air to settle. I want the blood scrubbed from the streets. I want to love this city again.

-Mae

◆

In The Year of the Queen
Found Tattooed on the Inside of a drugged Alchemist's Lips.

This the story of a heart.
It is the only story.

◆

The Collector is not wearing any shoes.

The Collector is not wearing anything at all. The Collector breathes big into new lungs. It has been a long time since the Collector used lungs.

At the Shore of the Sea Impervious, the Collector stands and arches their back. The Collector pushes dark, dark dripping hair from a damp forehead and pauses. Emerging from the Sea is tiring work.

Emerging at all is tiring work.

◆

1003 Years Post Regina.

There once was a snake who moved in only one direction. One day, this snake met a careless clown. The clown, desperate to bring cheer to a sad friend, took the snake and made it into a hoop to toss and distract her from her worries. They threw the hoop once, twice, higher, and the third time the snake went so high no one could see it. The clown waited and waited, until their thoughts became distracted. The Stewards would say the snake had fallen elsewhere, but the truth is that the snake remains high in the air, spinning and spinning, and still moving always in one direction. Will anyone catch it?"

I found this story written over the pages of a popular play on the day the clowns moved in to the huge abandoned building that would become our home. I found this written before I could know what it meant. Now I know, and I will do my duty. I have always been dutiful to my sweet old friend. I knew her before they knew her, before a crown made her head too heavy to lift. For all that though, she was my queen too. My queen, and my best friend, and the one who bought me my self.

I get confused now. I cannot tell when I am, but I do not mind. I have made the Queen laugh, and to return to such beautiful moments is not a loss. Solipsism. Looking back, I am sure it has always been this way, but of course that's the nature of these things. I wonder if I could make a joke of that, given I've become the punchline.

I have seen the Queen today, but she does not laugh as she once did. Her heart took root in an unlikely place and grew again after—after—after the bells. After the bells. I was watching the first time they rang the bells. When they ring the bells now, I remember that I could not save her, but I see her heart in the metal.

I have seen the Queen today, but there are no more bones in her hair. She told me it was time for the Night Carnival again. She has always loved the Carnival. Not even the bells could change that. So I will perform again for all the lost souls of the Continent, and her with me. She will eat their secrets, and maybe realize that the first secret she ate was her own. I wonder if, in that way, she knows how the cannibal feels, eating what makes you up. When they ring the bells that night, I'll forget that I can't save her. It is still worth it to try. To hear her laugh.

Love the laughter, even if you must lose the Queen.

The next time I see this room I will be you, and it will be the first time. It is a strange feeling, to walk out of the home you know, to meet a friend you love yet arrive to her as a stranger with no place to go. I think maybe that is the dominant motion of life, distilled into a choice. The laughter and beauty is worth the pain, and I will make that decision again. This I know for sure.

Once a clown met a snake who moved in only one direction. The clown had a friend, and maybe that's the only important part of the story. Once a clown threw a hoop all the way back to where they first found it. Their friend laughed and laughed, and she never much wondered where the snake went. The clown threw the hoop once, twice, a third time. Maybe the third time can be different. The Stewards might say the snake landed elsewhere, but the truth is that it's still in the air, just waiting on a clown to catch it.

♦

800 Years Post Regina.

The Archival Tower

Dim light.

Brightening. Becoming full: inhaling.

It is morning. The city floats.

Some morning. Not long ago.

There is a woman. She has just woken. She wakes, walks to the window, breathes in with the morning. Her lungs fill as the day fills with light.

She walks from the window to the door. She considers a moment.

She walks to the window. She gestures to all the things around her: books, scrolls, paper, bits of metal or wood, a desk, lamps.

The woman is silent.

Then.

The light. It stops, freezes.

From this height, at this time of day, the light freezes.

An hour. Two.

It is clear, a clarity that can only come with stillness. The city floats here.

Standing at the window. The woman. She inhales with the morning light.

Then.

She, too, pauses.

An hour. Two.

All things are still. No one is breathing.

The light begins again and the morning continues, inhaling the light.

It is the same every day, every previous morning: the woman wakes, walks to the window, breathes in with the morning, gestures, pauses when the light freezes.

Only when the light begins to swell again does the woman turn to her work.

Seventy-thousand such mornings have greeted the woman. Tomorrow will be the last.

♦

2 Years Pre Regina.

It had been years since The Mistress of Times could remember being surprised by anything.

Twenty years, to be precise.

She'd wandered into the market, listlessly regarding the trinkets on display, barely taking note of the performers juggling and dancing. She passed a stand selling elixirs, the same bottles she always saw, when one of the two faces she had sought for so long floated between the curves of pottery.

She stared as she had a score of years prior. This time, the beautiful face was a ghost of itself, lacking flesh and bone. It was Circe, nonetheless.

The Mistress slipped back into the shadows, scanning for the thief who had stolen her friend so long ago. He wasn't the merchant in the tent who ordered the ghost to fetch wares for the throng of clamoring people. The Thief's face was absent among the crowd.

The Mistress had found Circe, even if she was but a ghost of herself. It was a sign that her hunt for the Thief was finally coming to an end.

She would finally trade her bad times for future good times.

♦

1002 Years Post Regina.

The Narrative Opening to a Play Popular in the Lyceum.

The Tale of the Lost Keys

A tale is told that when the End comes, the ages will be reborn, the people reshaped, the land renewed. The old gods shall die and their seed planted to grow from the hearts that will be.

Yet still, from the quiet spaces between, some will rise that hold space, observe time, and serve the cycle as they ever must. And where there are spaces between, there must be Doors.

To every Door, there must be a Key.

Some have said these Keys were lost by the Stewards of the Floating City, outside of time, and this loss is the great failure that is whispered of in dark corners: a secret that should long ago have been eaten but is indigestible.

Others, who measure their days in steps of faith and hope, believe that the Stewards tossed away the Keys to save the Queen. Still others whisper of arcane artists, their madness guiding their hands to shape. Only fools claim to have dreams that the Keys were gifts of the Moirai, spun of fossilized silk from the vault of worlds.

Because they are fools, everyone listens to them.

Whatever the source of the Keys, their story remains the same: they are twists of fate that, if used in the right door in the Lost Continent, allow one to step into the Space Between and bypass the end of times—for a price that is known and a price that is not known.

It is easy enough to find a key; Shears of the Wyrd Sisters can sell you one at a price that is known.

Finding the door belonging to each key, however, is another matter.

Doors define spaces—we must surmise that doors of spaces Between need not be wooden or iron, but of moments of transition, comprised of winter and spring, water and fire, stones and dust, between words

or hearts

or ideas

or hopes

or fears

or prayers

or poetry

or loss

—each Key sings for a certain Door.

It is said that when the Key is close to its Door, a stunning chord shall resolve within the holder's heart and the passage made clear.

It is then that the second price shall be asked.

♦

"I do believe that if you studied a key, you could unlock the secrets to the door."

The Collector droned, mistaking their apprentice's long-lost stare for fascination. "This one, for example. The stone gleams like sunlight, so the door will show itself by day. The swirls that have grown over it? They remind me of violets—perhaps that means the spring, or even among a field of violets.

"I have heard lore of one expansive meadow on the Lost Continent where violets would bloom, vast waves of them. In the spring the pole would be erected among them, a rainbow of silk ribbons. The love-lorn gathered there, and the fevered dancing raced to the first gleams of light. As the light flashed at the horizon, they would discover what a twisted thing had become of flesh and silk."

"Perhaps the Key tells us of a Door shaped in that vernal ecstasy. Perhaps."

♦

1 Day Post Regina.

From the Queen's journals

If there were nobody left in all the world who knew your name, would you remember it yourself? Would you search for it in the mouths of strangers, breaking open their lilts and syllables like sabra fruits? Would you study the hands of lovers as they undressed you, watching, waiting for the moment they would know it, or you would know it, or somebody would know it, hoping it would escape from spent breath, skipping over tongues? Would you be sure you could recognize it if it happened? What would you do if it did?

♦

The Queen of Bones is dead. In the distance, a bell rings, and the sound grows fainter and further. Her eyes are closed. Her breathing is steady. She is awake, a hard surface beneath her. A warm weight on her body. Blankets. She inhales deeply. Metal. The air smells like metal. She does not open her eyes. If she opens her eyes, she will have to know she is still alive. If she opens her eyes, she will have to find a new name. Wherever she is, it is swaying gently. A ship. The sound of bells fades beneath the hum of the engine. She sleeps.

The second time she wakes, it is because there is no engine. Only stillness. It is time. It is time to know that she is alive.

The cabin she occupies in the dirigible is furnished simply. Beneath her is the cot where she has been sleeping. Next to it, an end table, made in the ornately carved fashion associated with the wetland artisans of the Lost Continent. It is a merchant's ship, then.

She is wearing only a white shift. Her dress is nowhere in sight. Folded on a desk, there are leather leggings, a tunic, a wool coat. Simple, sturdy travel clothes. Soft leather boots in her size next to the chair.

On the floor next to the end table she finds a thick hide satchel. Upon examining its contents, she finds dried meat, salted nuts, and bread. A leather pouch filled with gold coins. A small, but very sharp knife. Six pairs of stockings. A small sewing kit. An old round key. A compass. A necklace, the very same necklace she wore to her execution. And salted chocolates.

The Clown packed this bag. The Clown always had packages of salted chocolates in their pockets. She used to tell the Clown, *If you keep these in your pockets, they will melt.* The Clown never listened. But also, the chocolates were never melted.

Her eyes pan the room, looking for a lock on anything. The drawer of the table. The desk. The door to the room. There are no locks. *What is the key for,* she wonders.

In the corridor outside the cabin, there is no one. In the small dining room, there is no one. In the cargo bay: no cargo, no signs of life. In the gondola, there is no one, but the door is open. Outside of the door, out in the world, beyond the safety of the ship, there seems to be no one. She unrolls the rope ladder. She slings the satchel across her back. She descends.

♦

When the clown walked out the door, a hand caught it before it could close. A stranger walked in to the dilapidated building, regarding the dust with disgust. They were tall and tailored and wrong, the wrongness seeped from them how coffee seeps from a crack in your favorite mug: bitter and biting and awful, too hot to touch. If you looked too long at their delicate golden mask, you might have gotten the impression of comforts lost to the careless motion of the world at large.

They approached the single dimly-lit desk with a carefree saunter and, carefully putting their back to the viewer, pulled out a chair. A common printing of a popular play was lifted from the desk by smooth black gloves. Time passed as the stranger read the less common words written over the text of the play.

HUH. ENTERTAINING, BUT NO.

The words fall into the timeline like action. These words are solid and tangible. There is no room for interpretation or impression on your part, only the absolutely factual expression of the speaker's intent.

Allow the frame of your mind's eyes to pan around the figure. There are deft motions of the hands, a sharp tearing sound. A crisp, precise motion folds the paper, and slides it into a pocket. The stranger closes the book and places it back on the desk. They turn and directly face the observer, a faint glimmer from the lone candle flashes across the gold mask momentarily before the candle burns out.

OH HELLO. ARE YOU ENJOYING THE STORY SO FAR? I DO
SO HOPE TO PROVIDE YOU WITH. QUALITY
ENTERTAINMENT.

The stranger nods at you politely. Do not look into their eyes. If
you choose to follow them as they sweep out the door, you could
watch them peel a fresh orange as they whistle their way through
the streets and alleys of the Floating City.

◆

Eight-Hundred Years Post Regina
Archival Notation

> hmmm. Let's see. Where shall we begin today,
> my   little   friend?
> themanwalksacrosstheroom.looksatthepaper.
> hmmm. Yes. I have noticed that some things
> have   gone   missing.
> themangesturestoeverythingintheroom.   Heh.
> Maybe I am just old. Perhaps it is time to finally
> publish everything, open the archive. Let
> everyone see the truth. Eight hundred years it's
> been, the lifetimes of six Archivists. And you.
> themanwalkstothewindowandlooksout. We have
> woven Her story, kept faith, kept Her safe. At
> each ritual, we tell Her story. Each year, for new
> Stewards, we tell Her story. themansitsatadesk. It
> is the Story, more than anything, that is truly
> Between things—Hers in particular. Without Her
> story, the city would not float, and all the unseen
> walls would break down. I wonder. Would we be
> forgiven? Would they forgive us? No. We will not
> work   today.
> themanlooksatmehewalksacrosstheroomandloo
> ksoutthewindow.itisdark.

♦

32 Years Pre-Regina.

Circe was one of the few friends The Mistress had made. For centuries she had been wandering the world, back and forth through time, but never staying very long in anywhere or when. Her interactions with mortals were few, by design, save when she needed to bolster herself for her travels with a small theft of time. She'd lost count of the number who had accepted her trick: would you like to trade your bad times for good?

Without fail, people chose hope over sorrow, and The Mistress of Times was never stranded. It was far less conspicuous than absorbing all of their years, and some mortals' sacrifices could fuel years of travel anyway.

At a market one sunny morning, the Mistress found herself mesmerized by the performance of a girl dancing for a small crowd. The spectators tossed coins at her feet as the girl swung waves of waist-length black hair, her feet tracing well loved patterns into the dusty earth.

The girl sat to take a small meal, and once the audience dissipated, the Mistress approached. She asked the girl if she wanted to trade her bad times in exchange for future good times.

Circe was the first mortal to say no to the deal. She told The Mistress that every second of her life made her who she was, that every moment was precious. The Mistress mumbled a shocked reply and lost herself back into the crowd as Circe took up her dancing again.

As the evening settled in, the girl broke away from her group to spend some of the days' earnings before the market closed. The Mistress followed her at a distance through the alleyways, but lost her in the crowded twilight street. She heard a scream in the din of people and turned fast enough to see the struggling girl being dragged into an alleyway by a strange man.

The Mistress rushed down the alley after them, causing the man to turn back; the girl begged her to go get help. The man sneered at The Mistress as she asked him for his time. She touched his chest and stole his lifetime, the sneer was locked onto his face as he fell to the ground.

The Mistress hadn't used her gift in front of another being since she had left home centuries ago, sick of being used as a personal assassin. She was ready for the girl to look at her in terror. She was ready for the girl to turn and run. She wasn't ready for the girl to embrace her with gratitude. Circe took The Mistress' hand, stepped over the foul man's body, and brought her back to her family, who heralded The Mistress as a gift from the ancestors.

The Mistress spent ten years traveling with Circe and her people. They were a tight knit band of travelers who made their way from place to place. When asked why they had never settled, they told her that they were never welcomed to. They were always seen as outsiders, but they welcomed The Mistress even though she was an outsider.

She well earned their trust and used her abilities in their aid. When they approached a city The Mistress could go forward in time and find the days the market was full of paying customers. She could go a few years ahead and find out when the festivals took place so they could be there and ready with carts full of goods to sell. For once, The Mistress felt truly needed and loved, her connection to Circe as close as that of a sister.

♦

He clasped his grandmother's earrings in his bloody hand.

They are all he had asked after her death, and his sister Imogen had fatally learned that there was no bargaining on that matter.

How many evenings had he sat at Baba's feet and asked her again to tell him about the Keys she always wore dangling from her lobes? Some would keep Keys near their heart, but Baba said she wanted to see you try to reach for them. He asked the same questions every time.

What is the Space Between?

What do you mean, the door need not be a door?

Has anyone ever found a door and escaped the world?

Why would you want to escape the world?

The key sings, but what song?

So many questions, born of youth and hope—two traits growing scarce these days on the Lost Continent.

She had conjured stories for all his questions; as an adult, he recognized the ones that were mere fancy, changing every time she answered him, and the ones that were incantations. His Baba had dreamed of finding a Door; she wore her Keys her entire life until a final door did appear, but not the one for which she had sought.

He put the earrings into his own lobes. He would take on the same purpose that she had—for as long as his plague-infested spirit would allow.

♦

Year 4 Post Regina.

You can sum up every day like this:

A form stands at the window of the Archival Tower.

Below: the city.

From the window, the form takes one last gaze across the city below.

The morning has begun to inhale again.

This is the Archivist.

In a small chair, a chair made for a child, a clockwork sits.

It waits.

It does not inhale. Does not breathe

It is waiting for the person to speak.

It is far from the window, in the corner, in the shadows, next to the massive spools of paper that taper across the child-size desk, under the clockwork's small hands.

The Archivist simply has to speak. The clockwork writes what the Archivist says.

Everything.

All the Archivist has to do is speak.

And refill the inkwell into which the clockwork dips its quill.

♦

"It's strange," the Collector mused.

The Collector's apprentice stifled the same yawn he had stifled every morning of his indentured state. He gazed up with feigned interest at the dangling metal spirals, hanging from the ceiling of the rusted Binhouse like false stars. The Collector must have gathered these Lost Keys over centuries. The apprentice would learn to hunt them too, in time.

"The Keys," The Collector said, aubergine robes criss-crossed with dust lines mirroring the ripples of their ancient skin. They reached up and traced the sinuous curve of one twisted silver shape. "The shapes have begun to change, as though a great pressure of the Age bore down upon them."

"It must be a sign. But of what?"

♦

50 Years Post Regina.

Was she the First? She had not found another like herself, though what name would she give them if she found them?

The magic of a song is built of the same threads as a name. Names hold unspoken stories and must be cracked open to tell them—but a song...the magic of a song can be drawn out from a skein, slow unwinding loops that soak into skin like the memory of sunlight.

Both stain the spirit.

She found her songs long before her name returned. When first she stole this construction as her body, the taste of her birthright was impossible. Survival, shelter, secrecy. A Shape that would not be suspected. Escaping the Steward's Boundary was a year of the In Between, and success sent her into the first unsuspecting form—a clockwork smith crafting bells in Foundry Alley.

It was empty in there, ripe for spirit to take hold among the gears and wheels. How many years had her spirit been siphoned of its magic to fuel the alchemists' craft, and now a Bone Person made that craft her bones.

She did not have time to be bitter.

With form came the blossom of power that had once been the Gift of the people, and the curse that had put a glint in the eye of the Alchemists. Now it would be their salvation.

If metal can hold a soul, then can it not also carry a song?

♦

213 Days Post Regina.

The Collector cannot even find the palace. It has burned.

So much of the Floating City has burned. Blood is still being scrubbed off the stone streets. Windows are knocked out of shops. Down an alley, something small. A child, probably, scuttling into the shadows at the sight of the Collector.

In the distance, bells. There is a festival in the bazaar. Hundreds of bells are ringing. Large bells. Small bells. Shops have put bells on their doors. The people are wearing bells on their ankles and wrists. There is dancing, shouting, laughing. The people are drinking wine and aged liquor. The women have made an ale flavored with gruit.

The Collector makes their way through the crowds. Somebody puts a clay mug filled with the ale in their hands. The Collector drinks. It tastes floral, and a little like oranges.

Finally, the Collector stands within view of a stage. On the stage, a wax woman wearing a red dress is carried out by two upright clockworks with heads like bulls. They place her neck on a chopping block. A third bull clockwork raises a gleaming axe and brings it down on her soft neck. Her head rolls. The people cheer, thunderous.

The Collector drinks.

◆

Archival Notation
It has been nearly four years.
> *I do not know the day, but the anniversary is coming up soon. I found this: it is an advertisement for something called the "Spectacle of Bells." How quaint. Marked Artifact seven-two-one-three.*

Come Ye To

THE SPECTACLE

of

BELLS

To Take Place In The
MARKETPLACE CENTER
On The Eve Of
THREE WAXING CRESCENT

*Come! Ring In Our Fredome From
The Tyrannye and Diseaze Of
Osseaine With Thine Owne Bell As
We Execute Thee Elegante Waif,
BERTA, She Who Sought Once
Againe To Ressurect The Age of
Queenes! She And Her Cohorte
Shall Know We Haile No Crown,
And She Shall Be Lefte With No
Head Upon Which To Bear It!*

Bells Are Available To Purchase In The Foundrye District
No Bells Allowed In The Keye of D Minor!

◆

That night twenty years ago, the camp had been set up an hours' walk from the city. The Mistress had gone ahead to scout, and was already returning to the camp once twilight had succumbed to an inkspill sky. As she approached camp, she heard chanting in a language she didn't understand, and underneath it, horrified cries. A group of the family was bound, guarded by a handful of people in long robes. Several members of the family, including the family matriarch, sat on the edge of the encampment unbound, looking as if they were in a trance.

As The Mistress tried to wrap her mind around what was going on, she saw a third group behind the camp, huddled by huge ships festooned with wings and balloons. She again recognized the matriarch of the family among them and stared in alarm each person gathered by the ship was a translucent doppelgänger of those in a trance.

As if to confirm her fears, the robed people in the camp had encircled one of the men and, chanting one robed man reached down and pulled his spirit straight out of his body. An older man, wearing the trappings of authority, escorted the spirit to the group by the ships and gave orders to begin to move them aboard. She would come to call this man "The Thief" until she learned his true name.

The Mistress circled the camp as she saw them pull her beloved Circe from the group. A new round of wailing rose up from the group tethered together. She knew she had to act fast, so she silently stole the lifetimes of the two robed people closest to the ship. The tumble of their bodies falling to the ground caught The Thief's attention and gave her the opportunity to lay her fingers on him as well. His lifetime flowed at first towards her, and then pulled back, refused to obey her call.

He pulled out a vial gleaming with blue fire, which he dumped on The Mistress, immediately freezing her in her skin. He started chanting and a piece of her felt like it broke loose to be sucked into the man's vial. His incantations broke her from the frozen state, but her second attempt to steal his life had no effect. Try as she might, she could not steal his life away.

The robed minions had encircled her, and their chant froze her once more. The ghosts were shuffled onto the ship, Circe with them but still inside her body. The Mistress could do nothing as her only friend fought for one last embrace and was tossed onto the ship. The Thief laughed at the futile display of affection, bowing to her with the pointed words "Thank you for your time." He shook the vial in front of her face and placed it in a pocket deep within his robes.

A long while after they ascended with their gruesome haul, The Mistress was able to free the bound people. The family that had been on the boundaries of the encampment seemed unharmed physically, but they had no memories of who they were. They had no personality, they were just husks of their former selves.

At daybreak The Mistress left them, vowing to find the villains that had stolen the very essence of the family and her dearest Circe. She had walked timelessly for so very long, but now she finally had to count the sands in her own hourglass. There was no way of knowing how much of her gift had been taken, or how much time she had accrued throughout her travels. Either way, she knew that to find the Thief she would have to live as mortals do and hunt him down one day to the next.

♦

Some keys had no stone; the Collector wasn't certain if that meant they were defunct or merely different. Both options were ripe with possibility.

There was a place on the Continent the Collector would check every century, in the Wilds past Fieldtown where the lost bodies that no longer could serve the Establishment were left to go feral. These Keys were not the replicas crafted for taking advantage of Continent denizens desperate for salvation.

Gossamer Cave was untouched even by those who managed to survive the Wilds, for reasons that became immediately obvious: an untold number of clockwork spiders wove vicious wire webs that sliced instead of stuck. Here, spiders had found Lost Keys, probably on the hopeful dead, and used them as the base for their wire webs.

The Collector spilled much blood to extract a Key, but every price must be willingly paid.

Thirty-Eight Days Post Regina.

The Bridge City sits beyond the coastal swamps and is divided in half by the Red River, which displays rust-colored shores from above. The rocks and sand are a deep red color, vivid in the sunlight and haunting beneath the three moons.

Story goes, says the man with the mug full of ale, *the sand used to be white. A long time ago, before they built all these bridges, somebody petitioned the Nameless for a favor. A man was in love with a woman who didn't love him. He drank too much one night, thought it'd be a good idea to ask the Nameless to give him that woman's heart. So they did. Came up out of the river and plucked the thing right out her chest. Handed it to him. He was so sad over it, he carved his own heart out of his chest and threw both hearts in the river. When he toppled in, dead as anythin, all the sand and all the rocks as far as the eye could see turned red. Now it's the Red River.*

Is that so? Asks the Collector.

The man with the mug of ale takes a long swig and sets the steel tankard down on the bartop. *Oh yeah,* he says. *Everybody knows it. That's what you get for tryin' to make a woman love you. Either they do, or they don't, and you can't go cryin' to devils just 'cause somebody didn't do what you wanted. That's what you get for tryin' to talk to the Nameless. Everybody knows you leave the Nameless alone. Recipe for trouble.*

He pauses. He looks at the Collector, lowers his voice, and says, *My Nagyma knew things, you see. She's the one who told me the story was true. She's the one who gave me this.* The man reaches into his shirt to pull out a long leather cord. Attached to the cord is a key. An old round key, made of brass. The man sways on his bar stool. He is drunk.

The Collector pretends not to recognize the key around the man's neck. The Collector shrugs. *I don't know what that is,* says the Collector. And then the Collector waits, their slender hands folded in their lap. They sip from small steel cup. Sour wine made with a fermented fruit that grows in the swamps near Widows Bay. Some things about people do not change, muses the Collector. The way they will ferment anything they possibly can and drink it until they cannot sit upright, for instance. The last time the Collector came to the Continent, it was a small root vegetable they were fermenting. The result was bitter, but the people, they drank it anyway.

What're you passing through for, anyhow? asks the man.

The last time the Collector came to the Continent, they stopped through these cities when they were still villages, to grant a wish here and there. But time passes for people and other sorts of mortal creatures differently than it does for devils. The Collector had become distracted for hundreds of years, and forgot to collect the debt owed to them. The debt was less important than the task at hand, but the Collector thought that one might as well, if one crossed the opportunity.

I've got business in the Floating City, the Collector says.

Oh, you don't want no business there, says the man. *There's a war. Merchants stopped tradin' and everythin'. Folks keep comin' down here to escape. They got this new Queen, and then they killed her.*

They killed her? The Collector raises a perfect eyebrow.

Oh yeah, chopped her head off. Or hung her. Somethin'. The man draws his fingers across his neck in a universal gesture.

You know, says the Collector, changing the subject, *These bridges here are really something impressive. I bet you know the best one for a good view under the moons. I'm not from here, so I want to see everything I can before I leave.*

Oh, I was just thinkin'—what a good night for a stroll, says the drunk man. *I know the city like my own hand. Come with me.*

The two set down coins next to their empty drinking vessels and go into the night, the drunk man humming an old river song jovially.

The Collector had once picked up the habit of whistling, the last time they visited the Lost Continent, several hundred years ago. There is something about whistling that feels good. It accomplishes nothing. It serves no purpose, just whistling nameless melodies while one carries on, but it does feel pleasant. The Collector, standing alone on a bridge, whistles while holding the brass key on the leather cord between their thumb and forefinger. The Collector examines the key in the moonlight. Maybe it is the right one. There's no telling until you can tell.

◆

100 Years Post Regina.

The hammer fall may as well have been the smile of the Mistress of Times, so evenly it struck. It was its own festival of bells, the spectral clockwork smith mused.

It was a strange sensation: the new places that anger, fear, and hope sat, among the bones of clockworks. Gears. It had been over a hundred years since her soul had found a seat and she was still not familiar.

She wondered if her original body still felt the pains and pleasures of her life before slavery in the Floating City. Where did such things live, in the heart or in the flesh?

Another Key would be done soon. She remembered her father saying that you didn't know a song until you were tired of singing it. Now, she'd say that you didn't know a song until you'd bent it into every strand of metal you could ferret away when the alchemists were too busy to sense the hum, when trouble in the square drew the Stewards from their augury. When you rebuilt the song, note by note, from the history you could not bear to remember, and scratched the words on the inside arc of the borrowed brass ribs where your breath now lives. When you'd stripped your gears during twisting escapes, and must endure the surreal surgery of repairs to a host body crafted by your enemy—pretending all the while you are not an insurrection.

Then, you knew a song, even when looking through a glass darkly.

◆

38 Days Post Regina.

She stands at the first step of the temple, looking up at the arched door, which is encased by two stone pillars, the bottoms of which are carved with a pattern she has not seen before. Large circles interlocking smaller ones, it looks like. Behind her in the sand, a two-headed snake slithers past. Anceps, they are called. She turns her head and watches it continue on its way. She is standing too still for it to be interested in her. She has eaten these snakes; they are a delicacy in other parts of the Continent. Perhaps not so much a delicacy as a strange food people eat in order to show others that they are brave. Their undersides have tough, leatherlike skin, and their backs have hard scales, making them difficult to kill. On the inside, there are venom sacs throughout the body. If they are not prepared just right, the diner will die.

Beyond the temple, there are low sunbaked rooftops, and then mountains. Beyond, the outlands. Her heart breaks and breaks again against the desert horizon. She has walked 600 miles to get here. Before, she had never come to the City of Small Favors.

Before. Before, she did not go to the desert.

Today the small stone temple sits East of the city, roughly ten miles from the outskirts. If you want to get to the temple, you have to want it enough. Other cities have their temples nestled in their hearts. Not this place. The people here are too superstitious to have their temple inside the city. In some places, this may prove detrimental to visitors, but at least every time the temple shifts, it remains the same distance from the city. It's said to be built on one of the Beacons. Thank goodness for small favors, they say.

You might as well go in, somebody says behind her. She turns to face a young girl, perhaps ten years old, striding toward the steps with all the confidence of a wizened, grown woman. The girl's wide, flowy trousers are a vibrant red, and the color burns brightly against the desert backdrop. The girl is barefoot.

Aren't your feet hot? The woman asks. The sun is hot. The sand is hot. Everything is hot.

No, says the girl. She wiggles her toes against the sand. The woman flinches. She cannot imagine how the sand does not scorch the girl's skin. The girl takes the first step, and then the second, climbing the stone stairs without looking back. The woman follows.

Inside the temple, the air is cool. The floor is marble, and there are chambers separated with more arches and more pillars. There are more carvings decorating the pillars, the moulding, the walls themselves. It must have taken someone a lifetime to do these carvings. They are more patterns of circles, interlocked and placed against each other.

The woman follows the girl, who walks through the far arches into an inner chamber. In the center of the room there is a fountain, and the fountain is springing forth crystal clean water.

Nobody drinks the water, the girl says. The woman says nothing.

Through the inner chamber, there is a small room that contains an altar, which is a stone table carved with the same circle pattern as in the rest of the temple. The woman follows the girl to the altar and watches while the girl pulls a key from her pocket and places it there.

Who do people pray to here? Asks the woman.

Before the first compass was made, says the girl, *people used to find places by finding the four Beacons. Places don't shift on other continents. On other continents, places just stay where they are. What's North is just North and stays that way. Here, North shifts by enough degrees to make a traveller lost. They usually shift in the same sort of circuit, and the change isn't always very big, but the pattern is still unpredictable. So each city was built close enough to a Beacon that it stays where it is. They put rocks from the Beacons' sites in the city foundations to anchor them.*

How do the people know how to find the Beacons? The woman asked.

Lodestars. They are small favors.

I still don't know who to pray to here, said the woman.

A very long time ago, before the city was built, a traveller was lost in this desert. When they came to this fountain, they drank from it, and went to sleep under a sombar tree. When he woke, he found a child standing over him, eating a small red fruit. He was very hungry, and asked if the child would share the fruit. The child said yes, but the man would have to do the child a small favor. The man agreed eagerly, without asking what the favor would be. He was so hungry. After eating his half of the fruit, the child handed the man a key and said that the man would have to keep the key safe until the child returned for it. The man asked how the child would find him, and the child plucked one of the man's eyes from his head, explaining that they could now see through the man's other eye, and would always know where he was.

The man lived a long life, and grew old, and died without the child ever coming for the key. The story goes that when asked about his eye, he always said he traded it for a small favor."

The woman exhales and says, *I still don't know who to pray to here.*

Whoever you want, the girl says, and turns to leave. At the archway, the girl pauses and turns back to the woman. *What is your name?* asks the girl.

The woman pauses. She reaches into her satchel and retrieves two salted chocolates, individually wrapped in wax paper. She places them on the altar. One for the man, and one for the devil. *Regina,* she answers. When she looks back to the doorway, the girl is gone.

◆

587 Years Post Regina.
Believed to Have Been Written Pre Regina.
Found Transcribed in the Journal of an Ancient Alchemist, in the Ruins of the Manor Which Assumably Housed Him.

"I am not a writer, hell I can barely read. I feel the urge to start though, after what happened. See, I'm just a clown, my family travels from town to town putting on little shows to make little money. Last week, after a performance, I was washing up at the water's edge, and a naked woman flopped up on the shore. I assumed she was drowned, the way she just laid there limp, but I rolled her over and she was sucking air. We've been keeping care of her since, but see she can barely walk, she doesn't speak. It's like a fully grown baby just learning how to be. I don't know what her story is, but I'm pressed to find out how she came to be naked in the sea. She certainly didn't walk there herself, and I can't see whoever put her there being glad she's alive. Me and mine will watch out for her,

and I'll write down the story as it happens. It feels important enough to put to words.

*

Well here we are, it's been months but this woman doesn't seem to feel the passage of time, so I've only just now got much to say. She watches all our shows rapt, with the most simple smile painted on her face. Sometimes she laughs at my jokes or I'd wonder if she even understood them. She finally found her legs and since then she seems enthused to use them, so she dances every night round the fire till she drops. Sometimes she sings, but I still haven't heard a word. She sings like a bird that woke up with a human throat, but at least she's learning what it can do. She seems happy.

*

I never did put writing this down to habit. I guess what I realized is that even after you find a strange woman at the edge of the water the days just keep lining themselves up much like before. I still can't say much as to where she came from, she tells me there was nothing before the water but 'the Nameless.' She tells me they're coming for her one day, so I tell her we'll keep on moving. I guess what comes in the space between writings, between days, is life, and that grows a kind of love. She's my friend, somehow. I started carrying salted chocolates for her, she seems to like those.

If I can't tell you where she came from, I can tell you where she's going. Once she started walking, she started dancing. She sang before she spoke. She can spin a yarn better than your grandma after a glass of wine. And people love it, they love what she does on that stage. She starts performing with us and suddenly we're getting invited to fancy joints in big cities all over the place, the money rolls in like the river. So we're headed to some big stinking stage right now, in some big stinking city. Her first time in a city proper I imagine, but suddenly I get this feeling I've been here before. I just can't shake the feeling that this already happened. Maybe that's the real story she brought.

*

We've been in some City of Towers a long while now, and I'm getting restless. People are watching us awful close. I told her we were leaving, and she told me she wanted to stay. I'm certainly not gonna tell her she has to come with us; she's her own master. I just asked her about her favorite joke, before I left. I like to know what makes my friends laugh. So maybe this is the end of this story for me, maybe I'll never know who the Nameless Ones were. I hope she outruns them a great long time.
I still can't shake this feeling like I've done all this before, that I'll see her again, so I'll hang on to these scribbles just in case."

[Written below the transcription] "This 'journal' was found on the body of one of the mummers we harvested today. Their account runs parallel to the story the Queen tells. I'll be interested in seeing how the two respond to each other now."

◆

39 Days Post Regina.

"What shall we do without a Queen?" Their voices were lost things, half-broken trinkets leaking nostalgia like oil. "What comes next?"

The Collector felt their skin crawl as, underneath the cries, there began whispers like a dripping tap. Their ears strained to hold the thread of it, though it made their head whirr.

"I am the queen."

"I am the queen."

No one else seemed to notice, either rejoicing or lamenting in the upheaval. Still the susurrus grew, a hissed polyphony coalescing to a drone. It poured into a space between organic and mechanic, filled it, became the dew trembling between two wires of the clockwork spider's web.

"I am the queen."

"I am the queen."

"I am the queen."

"I am the queen."

◆

121 Years Post Regina.

Attracting the attention of a Wyrd Sister was a harbinger few wished to garner; fates tug on strings you did not know were attached. The skeleton fears rose up inside the brass shell of clockworks as I caught Shears approaching the back of the marketplace stall.

No one paid attention to a clockwork creature.

Shears did not wait for me to summon confidence to look her in the eye. "You're quite lively. You have something to trade, something worth falling for."

Did I betray my people by letting my thoughts immediately draw upon the keys I kept within the hollows of my gyrating guts? The Ancient creature laid a hand on the metal, cooling flesh against steamed brass. I could not tell if she could see me, or merely my time ticking away within.

"You will never spread them as far as you need." She rose to her full height, the glint of war in the spittle on her lip. "I shall see them into the hands of the People."

A heart I did not have stuttered to stay in rhythm at her offer. I glanced around but the denizens of the Floating City blurred as if they had never been there. All was foliage and branches and fire. A burning tree, a tumbling tower, a bridge between the sky and the land torn.

"I... I cannot pay you." Somewhere, deep within my memories, I knew payment would be important. Flaming stone fell all around, the cobbles ready to give way beneath us as fire caught onto the leaves nearest us, encircling. Perhaps she would throw me there, perhaps the threads would curl and sizzle.

Her smile was the crooked creature she no longer resembled. "This is a trade. The balance is made. You supply the keys, I shall find them paths to their doors."

The keys hung inside me, where they were safe. I'd only been able to throw a few to the wilds, my clockwork existence watched and waiting for an opportunity that never came. Shears could go anywhere, was made of the fire that would consume us.

I allowed her to scrape every last key from my guts save one. I needed one to remember the songcraft. The marketplace of the Floating City returned, with not a Fate in sight.

That night my dreams were as hollow as my limbs. I was certain I had sold one death for another.

◆

There was once a Queen.

And a clock-maker.

There was a morning a thousand years ago.

The morning had frozen, as it will again.

From this height, at this time.

An hour. Two.

A Queen. And a clock-maker.

- My Stewards. They wish to begin an archive.

-You think this will last?

-No-she added-That is why I want them to.

-You've taken their memories.

-No. I've given them mine.

-You think they will forget again?

-Yes. That is why I want them to.

-What do you want?

-Build a clockwork. That listens. That will write as my Stewards speak, it will write what they say.

The light began to swell. The clock-maker began her work.

◆

200 Years Post Regina.

She did not know about the first until she knew about the third, and it was the song that found her: twin voices conjuring up the warmth of campfire and earth, of the soft wetness that settled with the sun as she lumbered through the marketplace. She thought she would rust.

It was the day she learned she could make the clockworks sing.

It might have been a series of mechanical whirrs with pitch, but the spectres in their new shapes heard it and, where they had shied from her attention before, they swarmed. Once, it had always been like this: beloved family spreading like roots into every gathering, adults sharing wares, children sharing adventures.

Once, she'd been taught how to climb a tree; this day, she taught the free spirits of her people to hide inside these empty metal bodies where they could help.

Her new alchemist owner found her hours after when she should have returned, staring at the sky. Later, she dug herself into the song's memories, the taste of it blocking out a full examination conducted on her wires and cogs.

But Hope was not a Malfunction.

◆

248 Years Post Regina.

More have come through. We are all busy, too busy for me to transcribe these thoughts. It takes time for them to settle into the clockworks, for their souls to find seats where their power can flourish again. But when it happens, I can see it in their brass-lidded eyes. I worry, can others see it? Hear it? How long will these bodies serve us before the Stewards come to banish us again?

The Keys my family make are different but just as powerful with the magic of our People. The City bells ring again for another sacrificed Queen, and the cheers almost drown out my memories. Just as we rebuild ourselves through twisted metal, so the stories the Citizens tell begin to spin upon themselves. As they forget, we remember.

I have begun to shape my name once again, yet, once it is fully formed, I believe I shall bury it. I am no longer that being. The People will be the same and yet different, too. I don't know what we shall become, but we shall at least be free.

♦

The stranger meanders towards a specific manor, mostly in decay since the fall of the nobility so long ago.

OH YOU'RE BACK, I'M SO HAPPY TO SEE YOU AGAIN. DO FOLLOW ME, I WOULDN'T WANT YOU TO MISS THIS NEXT PART.

And so, you follow their trot, for better or worse. The pristine figure seems somehow in place here, juxtaposed against the ruined splendor of the ancient manse. The stranger adjusts their gloves, straightens their hat, looks directly through the fourth wall, attempting eye contact.

I THINK YOU'RE GOING TO LIKE THIS. THE EXECUTION IS MY BEST SINCE, WELL. THE EXECUTION.

The black gloved hand tightens around the door knob, and the stranger crosses more than a thousand years in a single stride through the door frame. Now we stand among opulence and revelry. Now sits A Woman, all in silk, with bones in her hair, across from the face of nobility.

"Now, let us have some entertainment," this face says and claps once.

And the Bone People enter through the far end of the room. And the Queen can be seen to subtly tense about the hands and face. The ghostly performers carry on in silence a moment before she calmly asks about the clown.

"Oh, they tell no jokes now it seems, but they do juggle and carry on. They came with the rest or I shouldn't have bothered."

She stands, and walks across the room. Her fingers brush hair away from a ghostly face, and nonexistent tears form on the idea of an eye.

"What's your. Favorite joke?" a tiny, tiny voice, from far away. Their lips don't move, their face doesn't raise.

Her voice is steady, with only the slightest edge of misery, "I don't think about jokes. I don't have a favorite."

The focus returns to the strange figure, standing just inside the door.

EXQUISITE. SCENES LIKE THIS ARE TRULY A ONCE-A-MILLENIA OCCASION: THE EXPRESSION, THE ARTISTIC RANGE. HER CONTROL BLOWS ME AWAY EACH TIME. TRULY A PERFORMANCE FOR THE AGES.
ON TO THE NEXT THEN?

♦

Year 2 Pre Regina Through to 12 Years Post Regina.

The Mistress of Times found her way to the Floating City. She followed the merchant and Circe through the districts to a large palatial house. The pair waited outside after being greeted by a robed figure. In the light of the moons, she saw The Thief's face as he gathered goods from the merchant and ushered Circe inside.

The Mistress set about learning the City, bartering time with the people of this strange place. She learned from the good people of Foundry Alley how to make trinkets imbued with abilities to hold time, to give time. She found a way through metals and magic to harness some of the power that was stolen from her, but part of her, the power to steal full lifetimes, remained stolen.

Most importantly, she learned the name of The Thief who had taken everything from her— a chemist named Khem. He deemed himself Master of the Harvest, keeper of the ways to create what were called the Bone People in the City. Khem had set himself up quite well, as there were noble families that used the Bone People as silent slaves.

The Mistress, usually preferring the anonymity of the Foundry district, found ways to learn of Khem's maneuvering in the City. He and his disciples were the only ones who knew the magic of the harvest, and he would pit the nobles against one another, fighting for who was most deserving of more Bone People. At strange intervals, Khem would cycle the nobles' supply of slaves, and the apparitions that left the noble houses to be 'refreshed' were locked into Khem's laboratories. Khem had kept Circe as his own servant all these years, and even though she was a silent shell of her former self, the nobles all wanted her as their own,for she was exceptionally beautiful.

There was one noble family that had a daughter Khem had his eye on, even though he already had a stately wife. The Mistress found out that Khem was going to barter Circe to the nobleman in exchange for his daughter Amalia, barely of age. The Mistress also learned that, though the noblemen in the City all had mistresses, it was unheard of for a noblewoman to become one.

The Mistress wandered through time, attending the parties Khem didn't so she could gain access to the family. The first person she reached was the nobleman's mistress. Much to her surprise, "The Queen of the Bones" was also not from the City, and was possibly the first person she had ever met that was also timeless. It became a connection between them, and amidst bits of forced performances and gallantry the two would share moments of truths. The Mistress provided news of the City, and the Queen offered news of the household. The two women joined forces to console Amalia, who wanted no part in being Khem's mistress.

The Queen and Amalia were able to cajole the nobleman into obtaining Circe as a show of good faith before Amalia was old enough to be sent off. The Mistress of Times brought Amalia and Circe into the tunnels beneath the Floating City.

Circe was a spectre of her past self, which crushed the heart of The Mistress of Times, while Amalia knew her family would have traded her for just a touch more prestige, she was broken by the loss of all she had known.

The loss of both Amalia and Circe was a spark among many rising flames, and distrust between the alchemists and the nobles built enough space for the uprising of the Bone People against their masters. The Mistress of Times remained underground to protect her charges, a ghost and a woman who wished for an end. Occasionally, she would hover under a street gate, overhearing proclamations.

The death of all the nobles, their children stolen away.

A great war that brought a Queen of Bones to a throne. (Her friend, the Queen of Bones? Could it be?)

Liberation for all, the Bone People released to the populace.

It was then that the Queen found The Mistress of Times again. The Queen wanted Amalia to become a protector of the city, to lead the other noble children she protected who would become the Stewards. Amalia seemed unable to contemplate the offer, traumatized as she was by her experience. Quietly, the Mistress of Times took the girl's bad times, soothing her. She knew the noble's daughter could not remain below ground forever. The Queen took Amalia away to the Lyceum, where she was made the first Steward of the City.

The city was in the process of being demolished and rebuilt day to day as different factions tried to assert themselves, it was only the Stewards that seemed to keep what little shred of order could be kept. The Mistress, ever wary of running into Khem kept mostly to the tunnels with Circe. When she did surface, she would hear tales of Emelea, the First Steward. Was this her dear Amalia? Did Amalia have so many bad times, that in the ritual she forgot the ancestral spelling of her own name? Could Emelea be any other?

◆

One Hundred Twelve Years Post Regina.
Archival Notation
My predecessor left this package. It is written, "Do not open for one hundred years."

> *"Twelve Years Post Regina.*
> *Archival Notation*

Amalia has requested time today. She says she has several artifacts to add to the archive. I will wait for her arrival.

- Yes? Please come in. - Master Archivist, thank you for seeing me. - Amalia, the honor is mine. - I will not take up much of your time. Here. These are for the archive. I no longer need them. - What are they? - Letters. - Of what sort? - Of the sort that need to be archived. But I have a request. - Anything. - Wait. Until I am gone. - Gone, Amalia? - Gone. - As you will. - Thank you. I will leave you to your work. - Thank you. - By the way, that is quite the view. The city is even more striking from up here - You are welcome to visit anytime. - No. I do not think I will be able to. I have much to do before - Before what? - Nothing. I have an appointment with an alchemist. I must go. - Of course. Let me show you out.
archival
My, that was a strange conversation. Perhaps it is just me and all my time spent talking with you, my silent companion. Well. Let's take a look at these letters.

Since I have started this archive, never have I torn a piece from the archival scroll. Now I must."

After she had gone? Whatever could that have meant? You were there. I wish you could tell me more, my clockwork friend. "Amalia." The First Steward. Ok, let's look at these letters.

Oh. I will read one of them into the record, but the rest will be archived and numbered.

Commentary on Artifact one-zero-two
"Dear Brother, Remember: Practice the Rites.
We serve the Between. But we obey the Queen.
The Floating City was once ruled by the six
noble families.
And the chemists, who have the magic to one
day make themselves forget She existed, served
them. Understand that She came between the
chemists and their noble families, and in doing
so, broke their rule. There was a war, fueled by
bottles of blue fire and magic that once made
slaves. Whatever She was in the before, she
became Queen in the vacuum that war creates
before the people can recover. Perhaps they
want to forget because the Queen, attending our
first rites at the altar, burned one of their
diagrams. We could not hear if she whispered,
"creation," or "destruction." She told us who the
spectres are. And we know the chemists are to
blame. Maybe there will be magic enough
someday to ask them where their bones are.
Perhaps this is why they hate Her. Perhaps this
is why they love Her. But never trust them. They
worship answers more than they do questions.
But we obey the Queen. We serve the Between.
Practice the Rites. Remember. Signed, Amalia,
Steward."

The other items archived, Artifact four-five-three,
Commentary on Artifact four-five-three, Artifact
three-one-two, Commentary on Artifact three-
one-two, Artifact seven-zero-five.

There is one other letter. I cannot archive it. I will
leave it on the window sill, and let the morning
decide what is to happen to it.

◆

385 Days Post Regina - Entry into the Logbook of the Temple of Condition.

An orphan sought our blessing today, complaining of cracks. He died before we could intercede, his skin splitting as he spoke.

What have we done?

Only what we were created to do.

◆

406 Years Post Regina.

The First, she has stopped making Keys. Since the Edict of Flesh, encouraging the hunt of noncorporeal essences, she has become very careful. She finds the Others who have escaped, whom she has set free, and keeps them safe until a suitable clockwork body can be found.

The rest of us have taken on the work of shaping our People. We have learned so much from The First. She encourages us to remember. The songs come first, carried in our ethereal essence. She sings with us, in whirrs and clicks and hums, and we begin to sing with her. There are so many of us now.

Other memories follow—the weight of bread in our pocket, the taste of sweet pimiento, separating the clothing to be washed upstream, the feel of the headscarf knot under our hair, the spying of a leaf to direct our way. These are now being shaped, too, into Keys to unlock the rest of us. They work, they must— more and more of Our People are coalescing into the City than ever.

◆

477 Years Post Regina.
Transcription of a Confession Before a Man Lost His Sanity.

Her finger was crooked with age, brittle yellow nail poking at the woven metal of the Key.

"Fools ascribe motherhood to the soft, the tender, building a perception of this transformation as revealing a white underbelly.

"But nothing could be further afield. The Mother is brutal, bold, damned. The Mother shapes life from the spittle of death, against all sense, outside of time. Mother is the intimate lover of cruel doorways and broken hopes, extracting from them their last inklings of possibility and throwing it up against the impenetrable void. Mother knows, and cannot ever speak, the truth of primal spaces: the breaths—and held breaths—between. That which is the egg succumbs to her, bequeathed both her protection and torture in the same ejection between her legs. A Mother fiercely guards her creation for her own private abuses, as General in the Army fighting Oblivion. The Egg is All."

The tiny suspended eggsac burst at the nail's touch, a horde of dust-mite sized clockwork spiders marching over her aged, cracked flesh.

◆

Pre Regina, Exact Date Unknown.

There are journal entries written on the pages of plays in the old building that briefly housed a number of clowns, jesters, jokesters, and mimes. There seems to be no order to these entries, but a clever observer might be able to follow them if they only knew the order in which the plays had been performed since the age of the noble families.

"It has been a long time since I have written, but now I feel like I can. I haven't been able to do anything for so long it seems. Now that I can, I'm eager to do most anything at all.

My memories are confused, I can't sequence them. I remember a strange man coming to our camp, and then it was as if a great barrier separated me from the events around me. There is a long patch of heavy grey, punctuated by what I assume were dreams. Visions of loud ringing bells and a carnival. There was a gallows, and a swordfight, and people cheering. Then I saw her face, my friend from the water. She looked sad even though I was performing; I tried to remember her favorite joke, but I couldn't seem to make her smile.

That's all I remember. Then there's a drum that floods me with fire and a familiar thrum in my ears. I guess I've been trying to figure it out since then, but I'm just so confused. I don't know what's going on. When I came to, my friend was there. But when she spoke I got lost in the bird song I had heard her sing so long ago. I don't know what came over me, but I just laughed until I passed out. Isn't that strange? I don't think she told a joke or anything.

Anyway, I have been getting a grip since then. My friend has been taking care of me. It reminds me of when she first came from the water, but our roles have reversed somehow. She says I should act like nothing happened, but I don't know how. Today I told a little girl a joke and she seemed so shocked that neither of us knew what to do, but at least I remember her name. Amalia. Such a pretty name. Maybe next time I'll be able to make her laugh."

♦

The Spectacle of Bells.

The Mistress attended the Spectacle of the Bells. She watched as the Queen was hanged, she heard the bells toll. She watched Amalia slowly harden in the face of the uproar. However, the Mistress had spent years learning the alchemy of time disruption. The collar on the Queen's neck had an aura of it. The Mistress was sure that the Queen would make an escape somehow. Her time in the City, if not her life, was over.

With a heavy heart the Mistress returned to the tunnels, having lost another of the few friends she had ever made. That feeling struck her to her core in a way she never imagined. She had never belonged to anyone or anywhere except the people that had originally found her and taken her in. She was found by the never ending waters by a nomadic tribe long before there was writing, but before mankind outside of the City lost their magic. The old wise woman of the tribe had taken her on as a charge and in gratitude The Mistress would go ahead in time and gather food or medicine for the tribe when it was lacking during the cold months when it was lacking.

The tribe was able to make a settlement due to The Mistress' abilities, but before too long, others encroached on her people. A battle ensued, and the old wise woman was pierced in the thigh by a spear. The wound was ghastly, and no medicine or magic would save her. The Mistress laid her hands on the woman who had been her mother and with a lilting nod of acceptance, The Mistress drained her time from her. Once she realized she was able to take others' future at will, she went after the warriors that had tried to encroach upon her people, and took each of their lives with a touch.

Without the old wise woman's care, the tribe kept her as a weapon. They put The Mistress in a cave to be utilized at their whim. Eventually she realized that traveling through time took some of the life she was allotted away, and the only way to keep going was to steal or trade time. She realized that she was just a pawn, as the people who had adopted her had died off years ago. Honestly, she had let herself die with the old wise woman who had been the only one to truly try to teach and love her.

 In all her years, she had only bonded with 3 other people. One was now a ghost of herself, one had forgotten, and one was now leaving the City forever. All that was left in her heart was vengeance and loneliness.

◆

The city floats.

And the nocturnes do not know how the morning stops.

It is somehow a little warmer at night.

A woman is sitting on the floor. Her back is to the heavy oaken door.

She does not remember how she, long ago, stole an axe.

Took it to Foundry Alley. Had a smith melt it down and fashion the handle and lock.

All she knew was that she had the key.

♦

311 Years Post Regina.

Unlike The First, I shall never forgive any of them.

I will never forget. Others have forgotten, but my anger is a burning thread that sews me to this world.

I remember when first my spirit was sundered from flesh.
I remember when I was shackled to serve flesh.
I remember when I fed the dreams of alchemists with my magic
And from the gifts of my people the gears turned.
I remember when we were the Key.
I remember when we chose the Queen, and she served us out of love.
I remember when Love was the edge of an axe.
I remember when we carved the path to freedom,
and the smoke from the temples swallowed the whole City.
I remember when we were the Key.
I remember when fear hung so thick that it begged a strong wind.
I remember when we dug a hole that demanded filling.
I remember when whispers became a direction changing gale.
I remember when they chose the flesh of enemies over the spirit of liberation
And the bones were pulled apart.
I remember when we were the Key.
I remember when the Stewards parted the clouds.
I remember when their love of the Queen clashed against ours.
I remember when reality shivered and the void came upon us
with only the Stewards as our fulcrum between worlds.
I remember when we were the Key.
I remember when we lost ourselves.
I remember when we lost each other.
I remember when the invisible became forgotten.
And I remember when we found the Key.

Now these brass bones will hold me only long enough to see the rightful paths of shame for all those who have sundered my People from themselves. I will see every stolen power reclaimed. I will see every invisible body in flesh. I will see every Steward undone. I will see every alchemist enervated.

I will see every thread to its earned knot.

◆

The Collector stepped over the dead man between the field row, examining the twisted key clutched in his liver-spotted hand.

Tearing through flesh with crumbling nails, they wrested the twisted metal from the corpse's rigor mortis grip.

This Key bore tassels that swung in the breeze; the field of wheat in which they stood bowed under the same wind.

In their hand, it did not sing. The field, however, whispered of their continued failure.

They stood for a long time, a breaker among the ocean of grain.

When they left, smoke rose from the blackened expanse and their irritation briefly quelled.

◆

112 Days Post Regina.

The Collector doesn't need a compass, because they know the Lodestars. The Collector remembers a time before people travelled enough to bother with the Lodestars and the Beacons.

Now, special compasses are made here, in the City of Towers, and exported all over the continent. The City of Towers sits nearly in the center of the continent, surrounded by bluffs and hills. The city reaches upward to the sky, and some of the towers are connected by hanging walkways, hundreds of feet up. The Collector crosses one of these such skyways and enters a cafe that boasts a glorious view.

The Collector orders tea, sits at a window table, and admires their new compass. They don't need a compass. They just like the compasses.

At the next table over, a woman sits fidgeting with her own compass. The Collector watches, curious. The woman is chewing on her bottom lip, and on the table in front of her is an untouched pastry. She appears frustrated. Impatient. She is dressed for travel, the Collector notices. Her boots are sturdy, but have seen some wear. On the floor beside her, a satchel.

Is there something wrong with it? The Collector asks, gesturing to the compass in the woman's hands. She looks up, and meets the Collector's eyes, pausing to be sure it is her they are speaking to.

Yes. I don't know. It just doesn't work anymore, she says. She drops it on the table in frustration.

Do you want to trade? Asks the Collector, holding up their own new, shiny, working compass. *Yours looks very old.*

I can't, says the woman. *It was a gift.*

Where are you going, anyway? The Collector asks, and then adds, politely, *if you don't mind my asking. I am also traveling.*

I'm not sure yet, the woman replies. *You?*

The Floating City, the Collector says. *I hear they killed the Queen.*

The woman shifts her body and looks away from the Collector. She picks up her pastry and takes a small bite. As she chews, she raises her eyes again to the Collector's and stares at him, expressionless. *Who cares?* She asks, her mouth full.

Well, says the Collector, *I thought I might find where they buried her. She once borrowed something from my brother. I thought I'd see if I can get it back.*

The woman laughs, and swallows her bite of food. *I am sure all her things have been sold in the markets by now.*

Did you know her? Asks the Collector.

Just the stories, the woman replies, dabbing the corners of her mouth with a napkin. She rises and gathers her bag and coat, preparing to leave. Pausing, she gives the Collector a nod.

What is your name? The Collector wants to know.

Regina.

Regina strides through the room, through the doorway, and disappears without returning the question.

♦

Hello? Yes? Who is it? – Please let me in. – What time is it? – It is important. – I'm coming. – Who. Who are you? – That. Is why I am here. – I don't understand. – You have things. Of mine. I left them here. – I don't understand. – Letters! Don't you understand? The old woman. With the bone in her hair. She told me who I was. I didn't need the letters anymore. But I am forgetting. – Let me call an alchemist. – No! Please. No. Just tell me. How long has it been? – Since what? – Since the only thing you care about! Listen to me! How long since the she was killed? – The queen? Quiet. Who are you? – Just tell me. – Two hundred years. – Two hundred. The last thing I remember was a festival. There was dancing. There were bells everywhere. That was a hundred years ago. The Centennial they called it. I need those letters. Artifacts you call them. Letters from. From Amalia. Or Emelea. – Are you saying. That you are over a hundred years old? – You are not listening to me. – You need to leave. Now. Thank goodness she is gone. Did you write all that, my clockwork friend? It is two-hundred and five years Post Regina.

◆

Shhh. Can you hear me, little writer? You won't tell on me, will you? Is that 'chivist asleep? Aww. Look. You are writing what I am saying. I know about you. Soon, you will write what you are saying. The wild woman. She told me. She told me everything. But not yet. Not yet. The boundary is too strong. But I have something for you. It is a key. See? Look. Shiny, and swirls. Here, I will put it inside, with your whirls and coggles. I brought it to exchange for some of the treasures you have here. Look. I found one already. The Wind brought it to me. I saw her grab it, from that window right there. There are others. Things I have found. I keep them. Good? Good. Shhh.

◆

603 Years Post Regina.
The Remains of a Burnt Diary on the Lost Continent.

*I found my lover dying of wonder one night. She lay in the
field, pierced through by flowers. "The door," she
crooned, the Key falling from her hand. She began to
cough. "I saw the door, but I stayed... stayed, for you.
It was bright. So bright..."*

*I asked her if it was like the moon, and she shook her head,
like her skull could not remain long on her spine. "It
was a universe of heavenly bodies, paying homage to
the seduction of the lustrous and the darkened. There
were many moons, and they turned their faces to bask
in the glow of their coupling."*

◆

Post Regina 1003 Overheard at a Pub, Half an Hour Before Last
Call.

*"Ya know, I seen this fancy dressed one in a mask around by
the Steward's Altar. I thought most of those types were
gone with the Carnival."*

*"I think that one crossed me in an alley by the old manor
thother day. Strange eyes I tell ya."*

*"Well I was cryin my wares out in the front courtyard there
and I sees 'em so I call out if they want a flower and
would you believe that all my flowers had gone to wilt
save orange blossoms? They bought every one. There's
Devils about I say."*

"There's no such thing as Devils no more than there is a Bone Queen. Just stories made ta keep ya up anight. Next you'll be telling me there's folks living in the tunnels under the city."

"Well I HAS seen folks goin in an out a there, and the baker I see tells me he sells loaves and loaves to some sprite living down there"

"You're in the sauce buddy, sleep it off"

♦

759 Years Post Regina.

The First has died. She must have. I, The Seven Hundred And Sixty Third Shaper, am told she climbed up the tower and never returned. One of us saw the remnants of her brass tossed into the reclamation bin—we stole as much as we could without being caught. Inside, rounding the inward curves of the husk that had served her for centuries, we found scribbles in our native tongue. Her fears, her hopes, and all that she struggled with in the beginning when she was The First and The Only, when she dreamed of freeing us all.

We shall shape these words into Keys as well—they are the bridge of our story, where the river has run.

♦

842 Years Post Regina.
A Love Letter Found in a Locked Chest Sold at an Auction, Containing a Key and a Note.

"For you, one world, one sky, one universe is not enough. My gift to you is a Key to all the cosmos in time. Every night sky splattered with stars that have witnessed

lovers' kiss, every whirling existence, every sun, moon,
and shattered dream I would give you, fasten them
like flowers into the ebony earth of your hair. For you,
I would pay the price to slip between."

◆

992 Years Post Regina.

They have mostly forgotten us, the Citizens of the Floating City. By the five devils, I swear their stories are more twisted than the reality. They have built a house on their fears, and it is grand and empty of anything other than echoes of who they believe they are.

It is an ideal place for ghosts to take up residence.

So many of us have escaped that there are not enough clockworks to hide our spectral forms. At first, I could not rejoice because my fear was so great that it would undo us. But the Citizens, whether long lived or no, have snipped all ties back to the acts of their ancestors. They see us and wonder, some have even taken up studying the spectres of the City. The haunts that the Edict of Flesh tried to drive out are now no more than beautiful, ephemeral things to marvel at and mostly ignore.

But do not mistake me. We are still Things. If they could wear us, they might endeavor to.

So, too, while we inhabit the clockworks. Most Shapers learn to hide the gleam of life. Yet some of us are unable to hide anymore, unable to feign lack of sentience. The questions begin, and we lose a Shaper to the Malfunction, as the Alchemists have named it. The scrap heap is filled with them, and those who dared fight back. Our mechanisms are not fit for uprising.

About a century ago—maybe longer? Time is wrong-footed here—those of us who had too deeply infected their gears with life began to disappear into the Wilds below the city. We have survived hiding like this.

But never has our secret escaped.

Of late the Alchemists notice more—they are less preoccupied with their mercurial maneuvers with (or against, depending on the winds that bear the City forward) the Stewards, and the Unnamed Figures that have guided them in the past have been long from the Unseen. Without these rudders, the Alchemists begin to turn their eyes towards us.

We have been fortunate for so long. They must not See us.

Perhaps The Fifty-Second Shaper is right, we must slow our work on Keys to turn our hands towards arms. We need to be ready for the next War. We must reclaim our names.

◆

Pre Regina, Exact Date Unknown. Found on the Pages of a Tear Stained Tragedy.

"The Queen says there is to be war. I have seen such horrors already, and she tells me the streets are flooding with blood. I do not understand. I feel I know what WILL happen, but I can't figure out what already HAS. I am so scared for her. I do my best to cheer her; she used to laugh so much. Sometimes I make her laugh now, too, but I always wonder if it is really just back then. Even as I write this, I wonder if I have already done it, if I'm just lost in some memory and really I'm far in the

*future. Really, it's after the bells have rung. I don't
know what it means for the bells to ring. I like bells.*

*The Queen found others like me, other people who want to
make people smile. She says she's arranged for us to
have a school, so I can teach them. She says I can stay
there so I can be safe, but I do not understand. Why
am I not safe with her? Friends keep each other safe. I
am excited to teach someone though. Maybe I will like
to see the school."*

◆

30 Years Post Regina. A Sheaf of Papers, Written by Khem.

*I did not survive the war only to become as low as these people.
How long did I wear those grimy clothes, hiding
myself among the beggars? I helped dig the graves
when there were no more nobles to kill, helped shovel
the bones in. I did what was necessary.*

*They will pay. I would make that slattern of the Bone People
pay, but they already hanged her. The Stewards will
pay for stealing my slaves right from under me, my
way back to prominence sucked out of existence.*

*Liberation has made dogs of us all. I had to strangle the guard
of this tower with my own hands. I have built
everything I have, from the ground up, all over again.
The only things they could not steal from me are my
genius and the vial over my heart.*

*And today, I have unlocked the secret of the power stored
within it. I have halted my aging, using a drop of that
which I stole from the friend of my slave. Whoever she
was, I should have thanked her more, for her Time
shall become my time.*

I continue to experiment, with the hope that I can distill down the skill of stealing the lives of others so that I may no longer need count my years.

♦

804 Years Post Regina.

The Archival Tower

The city floats.

There is a woman. She has just woken. She wakes, walks to the window, breathes in with the morning. Her lungs fill as the day fills with light.

She walks from the window to the door. She considers a moment.

She walks to the window. She gestures to all the things around her.

Then.

The light. It stops, freezes.

An hour. Two.

It is clear, a clarity that can only come with stillness.

There is a woman.

She, too, pauses.

An hour. Two.

No one is breathing.

The morning inhales the light.

It is the same every day, even yesterday: the woman wakes, walks to the window, breathes in with the morning, gestures, pauses when the light freezes.

Seventy-thousand such mornings have greeted the woman.

The clockwork writer is far older.

♦

1000 Years Post Regina.

Lost Continent Diary Found Under a Dead Body.

They say this is the first year the Night Carnival has come, that the airships have brought more than the usual merchants, the first time ever that such amazing sounds and sights have greeted us.

I have heard tales of a time before.

Most delighted in the arrival of the airships, descending from their satellite in a spiral where the Night Carnival opens like an unfurled dream upon the land. We all attended—it would be impossible not to, not when the drums called to us. It is an all consuming maze of wonder that steals up like evening mists. The old adage says, an Open Door is a way out, and down here every breath is seeking an escape.

Few would dare use that breath to malign the Floating City and its magical denizens, and it is dangerous for me to spill ink for the same purpose. With age, though, comes foolishness. Death would also be an escape.

The Continent was a child, unruly, unbroken. My greatgreatmother spoke of our people from before the Establishment rose. The Floating City sent traders and merchants, and even then the magics of that realm were evident in their wares. She said they were a beacon of possibility, sailing their way on airships with such marvels as had never been imagined.

But like any ship, the Floating City brought her rats with her.

My greatgreatmother spoke of some on the Continent who begged for that world, who vied for trading their skills and magic to be invited back to the City. She also spoke of others who kept themselves apart, who avoided the strange merchants—our People, though I should never admit that such blood runs in my veins.

It was our People who caught the eye of someone in the Floating City.

My greatgreatmother told us the story when we were old enough to dream of war. She told us of our secret lineage, and she told us that the Floating City was our doom.

Who is to say what is truth? Not I, though I can say that the martial law and strict code have been in place as long as I have lived, and I am nearing my two hundred and fourteenth year. Song is prescripted, and should your feet even stumble, you had better hope that none of the Overseers of the Establishment saw a pattern in the steps. So many ills of the spirit have spread that the Floating City sent the Night Carnival. It has become a beacon of hope for many again, a place where maybe they might find a cure.

I cannot find hope in such a place, not while this shame lays upon my shoulders. I shall attend the carnival and add another Key to my coffers, and then never attend again.

I can feel it in my bones that there is a Door nearby; perhaps it can lead me to a way to change what once was for a possibility of something else. I am ready to pay the price.

♦

Approximately 2 Years Pre Regina. Found on the Center Pages of a Classic Drama

"Something has changed. We came to the new school today and I found unexpected clarity. My students all spoke of dust and wrecked rafters, but to me the building was pristine, timeless. The shelves are filled with books on humor, and plays, and beautiful stories. I found a note, but something was wrong with it. It wasn't the same, it talked about my friend. It talked about the Queen.

Things can be different this time.

All the books have my handwriting."

♦

It has been eight hundred and four years.
Archival Notation

hmmm. Let's see. Where shall we begin today, my little friend? I apologize for yesterday. Themanwalksacrosstheroom.looksatthepaper. Let me see what I was rambling about. What is this? themanreachesforthepaper.beginstotear. I can barely make this out. Themanwalksacrosstheroom.readsthepaperinthelightbyt hewindow. It says, "The man looks at me. He walks across the room and looks out the window. It is dark." You. You wrote this? And then just now. You wrote, "The man walks across the room. Looks at the paper." Can you? How long have you been writing about me walking across the room? Themanwalksacrosstheroom.looksatthepaper. What have we done? Themanwalksacrosstheroom.reachesforthepaper.begins totear.

◆

1001 Years Post Regina.

Diary Page Found.

Gemma,

> *I cannot find Shiny. I've searched and searched, I'm muddy up to my knees. I miss her clanks and songs. I pressed the flower she gave me but it has crumbled into dust. A lady with an hourglass took it and now all I can remember is how Shiny's hugs were the best. I've cried a whole lot.*

> *I have found others though. They give me numbers for their names and I give them back real names. They say they will help me find Shiny. Rusty and Lumpy have been with me the longest, they said that someone tried to take me in the night but they protected me, they did. They even washed the blood off before they would let me hug them in thanks.*

> *I sleep inside Lumpy's chest now, he says where his heart should be. He sings me to sleep. At first, it reminded me of the haunted woods behind the clockworks factory, but now the song helps me forget the cold. I asked them where they were from, what work they*

were supposed to be doing, but they said they don't work no more. They told me that they open doors and lead people away, and that people would get mad if they found out. I won't tell. I promised, and promises are made of brass Rusty says. I tell you because I know you would not tell anyone, you are my gemma.

I miss Shiny. I miss my mother, but she may already be gone. And she has not come for me, and we are so far from the district now that I don't know where my home is. Shiny couldn't have gone this far out, could she? But Rusty and Lumpy tell me that this is where all of them go, after the Malfunction gets too big. Maybe that's where Shiny will get fixed, and everyone will be happy again.

I was frightened at first, but Rusty and Lumpy might be my home now, until we find Shiny and we can all go back to the district and live with you.

Your granddaughter, Cerilee

♦

992 Years Post Regina.

I realize that my writings are mostly about meeting people. When you live so long after losing your best friend, the best thing that can happen to you is to meet someone kind. I am trying to figure something out, but how do you document your progress through a puzzle that runs all the way through you? And so I write when I meet people.

Coyote has introduced me to a funny man today called the Professor. He seems to have a different notion of humor than me, but we talk for hours. I hope he will be a friend, though we argue enough that you'd never know it. Still, his presence brightens my days. My number of friends grows and grows.

Do you know, I am rarely alone now, I think. I spend my time with Oracles, urchins, Magi, clockworks, and more who defy categorization even from themselves. All the most fantastical people in the city love me and call me friend and yet, still I miss the Queen. She gave me the gift of a heart, and it is full now.

It is full, and I would trade it for her laugh. Coyote doesn't laugh like her. No one laughs like her.

♦

1000 Years Post Regina.

My relationship with the Professor has soured. Finally, a conversation about the spirit of humor has revealed him to be a coward and a fraud! Chrysanthemum hands indeed! Ridiculous.

My heart hurts. I think I shall go find Coyote, and ask if she has ever lost a friend. She gives the best advice.

♦

213 Days Post Regina.

Regina hands the Troubadour her leather pouch which contains what is left of her gold coins. The town is small, full of fishermen. There is just one alehouse.

The Troubadour pulls her hood back, astonishment crawling across her face. *I haven't played yet,* she tells Regina. *You don't know if I am any good.*

Regina sighs. She is weary. *I just want to hear words. Real words, I want to hear them.*

The Troubadour laughs. She laughs big, from the belly. When she is done laughing, she tells Regina, *There are no real words.*

Regina opens her mouth to speak, but does not. She waits.

All words, the Troubadour continues, *are just the images of words. They are pretend. If a real world were ever spoken, it would cause unknowable damage.*

Damage? Regina asks.

We don't know for sure. A real word has never been spoken. At least, not that anyone knows of, the Troubadour replies.

Regina leaves while the Troubadour sings a ballad about a thief who steals the hearts of lovers and replaces them with living birds. Regina keeps walking.

She takes her boots off when she reaches the shore. The stones are sharp on the bottoms of her feet. She removes the broken compass from her satchel before leaving the satchel next to her boots. She unfastens her cloak.

She peels off her leggings. She pulls her tunic over her head. She folds them neatly and sets them gently on the ground.

She walks.

The water is cold. She didn't come here to die, she came here for something else. She is not sure what. She walks until the water rises to her neck. Swimming is awkward with one hand closed around the broken compass, but she swims. She swims until she finds the current. She lets it pull on her. She inhales. There is a pulsing in her chest, stronger than a heartbeat. It is her heart, and it is not her heart. Once, she was only a heart. She does not remember, but she knows. Once, before there was a body, she lived here.

She lived here. She lets it pull on her.

When the whale swallows her, she does not fight it. She curls her body into itself. She sleeps.

◆

The Stranger sits across from you at a desk. The desk is nice, oak, stained, but the ceiling is low and the windows are covered by cheap shutter blinds. From the desk they produce an ashtray and a thin black ledger. From inside their jacket they retrieve a pack of cigarettes and a holder. Then, meticulously, they insert the cigarette into the holder and light it before acknowledging you.

OH, HELLO. I WAS WAITING FOR YOU. I WANTED TO TALK ABOUT OUR FIRST EXPERIENCE TOGETHER. IT HAS COME TO MY ATTENTION THAT A MISTAKE MAY HAVE BEEN MADE.

They take several long drags, recline into their chair, and make some notes in the ledger. They are obviously fine with dragging out this dialogue.

I SEE. MY CONCERN IS WITH THE BOOK LEFT BY THE CLOWN. I AM AWARE YOU HAVE BEEN OBSERVING THEM AS WELL. CERTAIN SOURCES INFORM ME THAT THERE MAY HAVE BEEN OTHER BOOKS. CAN YOU VERIFY THIS?

Several long drags later, the Stranger sighs in revulsion. They rise and pace the room.

EVERYONE ANSWERS TO SOMEONE, AND THOSE I ANSWER TO DEMAND TO KNOW. HAS THE CLOWN WRITTEN ANYTHING ELSE THAT MAY INFORM THEM OF FUTURE EVENTS ON THE TIMELINE?

The stranger turns from you a moment and braces their hands on the top of a filing cabinet. You can see them breathe heavily. They shake their head once and turn again to face you. You see their eyes.

YOU CANNOT DEFY ME, I AM INEVITABLE. I CAN MAKE THIS VERY UNPLEASANT FOR YOU, BUT THAT WOULD BE UNPLEASANT TO ME.

...

"NO ONE TALKS, EVERYONE WALKS?" REALLY? CHARMING, TRULY A CHARMING READER, YOU ARE!

The Stranger storms out the door of the small room and slams it behind them. You certainly wrinkled their trousers, didn't you?

♦

60 Years Post Regina.

For two score years, The Mistress of Times was cut adrift from what was happening in the streets above her, save searching for Khem. The people of the City believed him dead, but The Mistress suspected that if he had perished her powers would have returned to her.

The Mistress was living a life in hiding with the ghost who just stared off mutely. Every now and again Emelea would wander into the tunnels and find them, less out of desire than muscle memory. The Mistress could see the years etching their way into Emelea's face. The older Emelea got the more she forgot, but she also started remembering things forgotten so many years ago. The Mistress couldn't take watching the last person she cared about slowly blink out as mortals did, so she hatched a plan.

One day Emelea wandered into the tunnels ranting about Khem the Harvester, how she hated him but couldn't remember who he was. The Mistress offered to help Emelea remember. Emelea resisted, but still took the cup The Mistress offered her. The wine was thick with sediment, but Amalia drank from it and listened as The Mistress finally told her the full story of Circe and Khem and how she came to be in the City. When the liquid was gone, The Mistress refilled it so that Emelea would drink of the dregs of the cup, not once but twice. As Emelea drank and listened, she felt her rage growing where sorrow once leadened her spirits. Her anger bolstered her, vigor returned to her limbs as quickly as the wine turned her cheeks red.

"It's a shame no one knows if Khem is truly dead or alive. Maybe one day he will be found and pay the price for his sins," the Mistress sighed as she poured another glass of thick wine. Emelea eventually stumbled off into the night, full of wine and the sands from The Mistress' hourglass. As the Mistress fell into the first peaceful sleep she had in 70 years, she couldn't help by laugh to herself. *'The fates have been cruel to us, but there is one whose touch I have resisted all these years. I have made another timeless one, Shears be damned.'*

♦

728 Years Post Regina.

Today I met a little girl who was not a little girl. She told me her name was Jovelette, and certainly she could not be who I remember her being. I know what they did to Amalia, I saw it all over again today. Made her laugh this time though.

What is really interesting about Jovelette, is that I remember going to the Continent with her. I remember a carnival, to fight the sickness spread by a government that doesn't exist yet. I remember dancing with her in an airship, sneaking out of the city together. I remember Jovelette from 1002.

There is something wrong with time. When I pick at it, it flakes away.

Today I caught Coyote singing bird songs. She even knows the bird songs. Some days it feels like the Queen is not dead at all—until I hear the bells.

♦

1002 Years Post Regina

There is a man.

And a woman. They walk next to one another.

There is a door that has not been locked in two hundred years.

There is a door that has not been opened in two hundred years.

Not since the disappearance of the last Archivist.

There is nothing left to archive.

The man and the woman open the door. They walk into the Archive of the Stewards.

They were sent to collect the archival scroll because, of course, they were Stewards. And to make ready the archives and artifacts to be open to the public.

A large table dominates the room. Under the dust are several letters. There is a note.

it says, "First."

They have a conversation. We may presume that they talked about how they were going to go about their task. Or about the dust that would have settled after two hundred years. They may have spoken about a tiny chair and desk, almost too small for even a child, sitting in the dark corner.

There is no one there to write down what they say.

The last words on the Archival Scroll:

I did not choose this role—well,I did—but I didn't know what I was getting myself into.

I signed up for what I thought would be a great cause: The Queen. A person to be served. Worth what I knew as love at the time, even 600 years after her death. Service to her was service to others. Service became obedience—but I could not tell the difference. I went mad.

My hair fell out and my eyes sank in. My cheeks narrowed and my gut rotted. I became something less human. More in between death and life—but all the time wanting to be alive.

Pouring through these archives, I began to see her greed and consumption of what should have been lovely. What could have been beautiful. But she mangled it—marred it—and lashed about. And I couldn't stop. I just obeyed. Weakly. With what little magic she had not yet drained.

And that's what I did. I failed. Like a raw diamond feeling "not as beautiful" as their perfectly molded cousins.

I studied. I grasped for truth. I asked the questions and found the possible answers—knowing there wasn't a single one;there were many facets. Many "could be's."

So she died. And we lived. And I exhaled so that I could truly inhale.

And for this—I now make up for it. For I breathe the air of reality—outside of her reign. I study the connections of what was or what is or what could be. I see. I see possibilities and could-of-should-of would-of's. And I note them. I archive them. I hold records.

But even now—I struggle with obeying the connections rather than maintaining them. For that is my curse from the time of the Queen.

◆

YOU DID THIS. YOU FORCED MY HAND. NOW I'LL HAVE TO BE MUCH MORE DIRECT. YOU'VE RUINED THE FINESSE.

The Stranger moves briskly down an alley toward the Foundry District. Their orange blossom lapel is bruised and limp. You are following them, which proves you're braver than I am.

SHUT UP AND LET ME WORK.

They reach a chess board and rip time wide open to step through into a dusty room. In the room stand two clockworks, the Jackdaw and the Coyote. The clockworks gesture, and hiss, and click. All the motions of a conversation you can't follow.

THERE'S GOING TO BE AN EXECUTION, YOU HAVE TO STOP IT. I CAN OFFER A NECKLACE AND A WHALE, PRICE TO BE DETERMINED. I'M NOT IN A BARGAINING MOOD, I HAVE TO MEET WITH THE CLOWN STILL.

The room stands silent. Dust settles on the Stranger's coat.

◆

300 Years Post Regina.

The Mistress and Circe were walking down the deserted moonlit streets. The Mistress had long ago given up on finding her old enemy, he had to have died two hundred years ago. Still she was like her ghost friend, haunting the tunnels of the city by day and the streets by night. They were about to pass into a part of the Menagerie district they didn't frequent often. The Mistress crossed the street and was half a block away before she realized Circe wasn't by her side any longer. She was staring into the distance at a Specter looming in a nearby doorway. The Mistress wandered over to the object of Circe's attention, and in doing so caused Circe to move again. Circe approached the other Specter and they stared into each other's eyes for a long moment. They started to hum. It was a song the Mistress had almost forgotten from those long ago days with Circe and her family. When The Mistress finally got to the door, she drew a sharp breath. The Specter was none other than the Matriarch of the family, Morgiana, who had been harvested. The Mistress guided both of them back to the tunnels while they hummed intermittently. How many more of the family were wandering this city?

♦

1002 Years Post Regina.

"What did you get?" He unwrapped the package with such delicacy, as though he were tatting lace from the thread of his desires. I smacked his arm with impatience, distressing several spectres floating by. "Come on, what is it?"

"It's from Jet." As though everyone couldn't tell the smouldering sourced from that ember. I pretended not to care, but loneliness must muster what crumbs of love it can find and I wound up right next to him as the box opened. A metal hand burst forth, and he laughed as I jumped clean out of my clothes. It was merely a casting that held a braided leather thong. A fancy display, but we both grew quiet at the talisman attached thereto.

A bone. Part of a rib perhaps? It's slender lines pinched to a fanning end, like a chisel. He slapped my hand away, already looking for the symbol himself. It was there, a brand of quality.

A bit of the Bone People.

Of course, as an old enemy, many children's stories were made of the Bone People. Fables were bolstered by the many bones that have been unearthed, from that time and before, that were surely the remnants of an enemy conquered.

But the histories tell of a war where they were destroyed, these exotic beings of bone and sinew and little else. The lack of skin allowed their magic to flow more freely, straight from the blood and bone of their purpose—to take the Floating City for themselves.

The Bone People didn't know: the Floating City would suffer no queen. They swiftly learned, according to the tales, and their hubris was their end.

Gifts of Bone are treasures now. They are rare and tout a bit of history, displaying your patriotism to the City. A piece of the enemy to remind people of what they could expect at the Spectacle of Bells. Jet would have had to trade something dear for this piece, which now warmed Paaris' breast.

It felt powerful to look at, to be reminded of those times when the Districts were forced to bow. Who knows what magic could be in it, from the days when magic was more wild. Perhaps it was possessing me—who could say what drew my hands to his neck.

Is this how they fought them, those criminals, with tooth and nail and blood and bone? Chancing everything, even friends, to save the True Design of the Floating City, a capital without crowns?

◆

One Day Pre Regina, In the Year of the Queen.

The majority of a feel good comedy is filled with the following words:

"I have been consorting with a very clever Jackdaw. We are hatching a plan to save the Queen. The execution is in the morning. I could not anticipate the acceleration of events up to this point, and a clown can do little to

alter happenings like this. I think I've done well, considering. Considering I was at her side when they crowned her. Considering I was there when the Alchemist returned, and when he left. All through the loss that followed, I did my best to make her smile. To feed her salted chocolates, as if that could soothe her pains.

Her pains though are the kink in our plan. The mechanists have given her a clockwork to eat the pain, eat her secrets and stories. I have watched my Queen feed herself to a Coyote. Jackdaw is working on Coyote, they meet in secret. If Jackdaw can't convince Coyote to sneak her out, I'll just have to stop the execution myself. I don't know if I can die, but I know I spent a thousand years wishing to change this moment.

When I left the Queen, I held out both closed hands to her, and told her to pick. Her first pick was empty, so I showed the other. Empty too. Oh well."

◆

SO HERE WE ARE AT THE EXECUTION, AND I HAVEN'T BEEN ABLE TO FIND THE CLOWN. THEY'RE A TEMPORAL ANOMALY, YOU KNOW.

DO YOU EVEN KNOW WHAT THAT MEANS?

I'M GOING TO HAVE TO DO THE SPELL. WHY DON'T YOU GO WATCH THE CLOWN SINCE YOU LIKE THEM SO MUCH, I PROMISE I'M NOT DOING ANYTHING IMPORTANT.

Your perspective shifts across the city in an abrupt jerk. The Queen is at the Altars, it is the day of the execution. There is a seething crowd, and off to the side, alone, there is a clown. The clown runs towards the gallows, but after three long strides they hit a wall of solid air, hard. The color has drained from their face. There's a hum in the air, and everything has an awful, sick texture.

"Listen to me you have to ---- ----!" The clown screams, their plea to end the atrocity sucked from the air into unutterable silence.

The crowd shifts to look at them, as they struggle against the solid wall of certainty blocking their progress. The clown makes to lift an arm in rage, they shout "Save your -----! This is -----!"

Whether it's wrong or not, it's apparently happening, as determined by the Stranger's entrance to the scene. They seem to be muttering, and their appearance has regained that utterly unlikable, immutable trait. Certainty, undeniability, leaks from them. The crack in the favorite mug grew and grew, and now it has shattered. The wrongness that seeped out the edges has spilled all over the ground and burned your hands.

Metaphorically, of course.

KID, LISTEN. THIS HAS TO HAPPEN. I KNOW IT'S HARD. BELIEVE ME, I KNOW.

The color has completely drained from the clown's motley. The Red and Blue of the Queen replaced with Black and White. "That stranger is manipulating us! ---'- you s--? They're a D-v--!" The clown takes a step toward the stage and hits another wall. A bare handful of people were still paying attention to the clown at this point.

"I knew those clowns were off, trying to interrupt the entertainment," answered an unkind voice from the crowd.

"---- are y-- do---? W---'s -ap---ing?"

EVERYTHING WILL OCCUR AS IT HAS ALWAYS BEEN. YOU WILL NOT CHANGE THIS COURSE OF EVENTS. I KNOW YOUR NAME.

And then the Queen fell. The bells rang, and the crowd roared out of general malice. The bells rang and rang and rang, and then the clown punched the stranger square in the jaw, as hard as they could.

The stranger fell down, and the clown laughed so hard that they fell down too. Isn't that strange? No one had told a joke or anything. The clown laughed and laughed until tears ran down their face, and then they were just crying. Ugly and dirty on the ground.

UNBELIEVABLE.

♦

1003 Years Post Regina.

Foundry Alley is a cacophony preparing for the Spectacle of Bells. Someone's clockwork peacock pecks at a large bell that is to be hoisted over the Oasis for the occasion. The smaller boxes, stacked atop each other in the wagons, jingle as spectres play with the bells meant to be sold to audience members. Who can slap a spectres' hand? The merchants grumble at the incorporeal nuisance, but I laugh.

In Two Days, we shall hang a Queen.

Everyone wonders who it will be this year. Last year our mock murder was a dancer from the Menagerie district, gown bedecked with ribbons, such that when she dangled, her ribbons fluttered like wisps of blood. It was the best Spectacle we've had in the last few years.

We must have our traditions. A story dies if it is not shared.

Sometimes it dies even if it is. That's where I come in.
Sometimes you need to exhume the corpse and make a new
story from its bones.

As though summoned by the thought, I recognize the aubergine
robes across the way and duck down. The Collector has arrived
for the festivities.

Early.

Agitated.

I gesture. Across the square, I see the return gesture. The news
will be passed among the others.

It is time; the clockwork pulls the cart past me to join the
merchants preparing their caravan. It is dull metal among the
whimsical attire that is the fashion of the Spectacle. As hoped,
the merchants ignore the clockwork as someone else's problem.

Soon, it shall be a problem for all of them.

Again, as though summoned by my thoughts, I see a face in the
crowd—a face I recognize. A problem face. A face that would
ask the location of my soul and I might smile to hide the citrus on
my breath. By the Stewards, her face is still as sweet as neroli.

There is no one to give a signal to; there is no signal for this
possibility because it was not possible. I gawk as the caravan
rolls away. She follows it, and no one sees her, not like I see her.
She blends in, as though she has always been here.

Sometimes stories don't even die when you hang them.

◆

The clown awakens in an alley, with two clockworks standing above them. They roll over and start to weep. The Stranger kicks them lightly in the shoulder.

GET UP. SHE'S AWAKE.

The Stranger bodily lifts the clown from the ground and leads them towards a cart.

ALRIGHT COME HERE YOU MESSY CREATURE. I'D JUST LIKE TO SAY, I CONSIDER FIST FIGHTS VERY UNPROFESSIONAL. I'VE NEVER COME TO BLOWS, NOT ONCE IN MY ENTIRE CAREER. YOU *HIT* ME.

They were standing by the door of the open cart, when the clown looked up into the face of their friend. Her throat was red and bruising already, but she was smiling at them. They stepped into the cart, sat down. Held out both hands, closed into fists. She picked one, and it was empty, so they showed her the other. Empty too.

"Oh well."

IT'S RUDE TO EAVESDROP. GO AWAY.

◆

Not Found At All.

"I'm writing to say that I'll never read this. I packed the Queen a bag, and I watched her leave. I have to stay in the city for a thousand years, and I have to think she's dead. That's why I come back after those thousand years and make tonight happen. Inconvenienced

strangers aside, I think I did quite well. She's alive,
she's really alive.

So *I'll take all my writings and burn them at the Altar, to*
destroy my memories again. I'll hope I'm not so clever
next time, and I'll spend the next thousand years
writing plays. That should leave me with something to
read for next time. There's no time at the old clown
school after all."

♦

213 Days Post Regina.

Coyote, the clockwork, wakes up and Sees for the first time.

♦

Post Regina 550, Written In The Authoritative Book of Jokes,
53rd Revision – Annotated Edition.

She has been gone a very long time now. It feels strange to
write again, and I find I have no blank paper. Most of
the other clowns have left or died or gone blank by now
though, so no one will miss this old book. There's not
much call for us it seems, and when the other Bone
People began to diminish, it was easier for the others
to leave I think. Kallidar tells me that I won't go that
way, on account of my Pulse. I don't know what that
is, but they have good sense.

Oh, about Kallidar. I've taken to wandering the city you know,
to pass time. Sometimes I make people laugh. I missed
that in all my years hiding in this old school. I met
Kallidar because sometimes I find myself confused and
lost, you see, and they found me crying by the Altar. I
do not know if Kallidar has friends, as they are from
the Moon, but I do have friends and I believe they are

one. They excel in the use of Capital Letters, which I find exceptional in spoken conversation.

I'm actually here to write about another friend, though. There was a time when I only had the Queen to call that, but she brought people together. Now I have many friends, thanks to her. Coyote was the first friend she helped me make, I think, but my memory is a blur around the bells so I cannot say.

I was with Coyote though, the other day, and something striking happened. I held out my closed hands to her, to make her pick one, and when they both turned out empty she looked right into my eyes and she told me "Oh well," and I swear it was the Queens voice. I swear it was the Night before the bells rang. I swear there's something else I can't remember.

So I'm not actually writing about Coyote, although I am. I'm writing about the Queen, the same as always. If only I could somehow go back.

♦

950 Years Post Regina.

The group suddenly went silent and still, a sure sign she was back again. Emelea, or as she was now called, Jovelette, entered the chamber. If she noticed that the group of Specters had grown, she didn't show it. In fact, she never seemed to notice them at all. She simply approached the Mistress of Times and said, "I saw the blue fire coming from a window high in a tower near the Oasis. I haven't seen blue fire since the war. No one leaves or enters that place, it is impenetrable. But, if I am still alive by your machinations, he could be too." With the mention of him the twenty odd Specters in the room started to slowly moan in unison. Jovelette turned and left for the last time, having finally fulfilled the suggestion the Mistress gave her on the night of her making. Jovelette was finally free to live her long years in solitude and never have to see her maker again.

The Mistress looked around the room. The family had calmed down again. Some started humming again. It had started when Circe recognized Morigana, but over the years they had found all of the family that had been harvested. The family was again a family, and even though The Mistress hadn't met the cousins while she lived with them, they found each other in the lonely streets of the city. Every time they had found someone they had known in life they acted the same: drawn to one another, they silently stared at each other and then began the low humming. The more their numbers increased, the more lively they were. The Mistress had seen Circe silently laugh. One of the boys had danced two years ago. The family was finding each other. They were waking each other up. And best of all, if Jovelette was right, The Mistress was finally going to get the revenge she had been starving for.

◆

1002 Years Post Regina.

Tonight was my first time performing with the Carnival. Coyote took me with the others to the Continent, to bring people joy.

I have never been so happy in more than 1000 years. All the citizens came and told me of the lies they needed to get through the day. Some made my heart ache, and some made me laugh. I think though that when everyone walked away, they were a bit happier. A clown should help people be happy.

I danced with the Clockwork Lemur while people clapped and cheered. Kallidar and I stole the Professor's cane to bother him, but I ended up tied in a knot with it, and Kallidar had to help me so I wouldn't fall. I have never seen so many happy faces.

At the end of the night, Coyote even introduced me to a Chicken, who wants to be a clown! I would so love an apprentice again after all these years. I would so love a future I wouldn't trade for the past. For now though, there are Carnivals.

I'm close to finding her again, I know it.

◆

"Threes are very important, you know. The phases of life, the phases of building life, the three parts of the mind...we naturally see things in threes, a beginning, a middle, and an end.

"Whenever I see two, I look for a third. Perhaps between those two lovers, the third is their union. Perhaps between two trees, there is a window of space unique to that place. Between two enemies, a war. Between flesh and bone, a soul. Between a Devil and a pearl, Hunger. Between a Key and its Door, a price.

"There is always a third."

A rusted arm opened a port hole, the tunnel flooded with blinding light. When their eyes adjusted, it was there as was promised—wisps of cloud passing to reveal a vast land below. "You see the Lost Continent, yes? And here we are, hidden beneath the Floating City. What is the third, my child?"

"The Night Carnival," hissed the clockwork child, its lens widening with impossible wonder.

◆

1003 Years Post Regina.

*I asked Coyote her favorite joke. Do you know what she told
me? I knew what she would say before I asked.*

*She said "I don't think about jokes. I don't have a favorite,"
and she looked at me like she was so confused.*

*I have never seen her confused. I don't have time to figure it
out anymore though, I learned about a Mistress of
Time at last year's Night Carnival. I'll seek her out
this year, and I'll trade her whatever it takes to go
back and have my time with my friend again. It is
cruel to go on so long after the loss. I can't wait to meet
everyone again.*

*I've been thinking about the note I found the night we moved
in, folded up all crisp on the desk, right where I'm
writing this, actually. There once was a snake who
moved in only one direction, until it came upon a
clown...*

♦

Appendix

Forty Years Post Regina.

Most Honorable Survivors of the Alchemists Quarter

Do you still not believe? Especially now? Indeed, it was your prescription to begin with, so long ago.

Y(our) gods were beautiful—design given face, possibility made emblem, distant and abyssal concepts rendered recognizable and traceable. We adopted them, indexed them, archived them—does this surprise you? Perhaps you meant them temporary, crafted for a necessary moment, but then they appeared at the Temple of Condition, standing before us, desiring not worship but merely to be looked upon (was this intentional in your crafting?) with names you gave them:

Dlethlan, of Under.
Glor, of Roads Leading Nowhere.
Kliph, demon of Breathless Pause Between Words.
Jorshaq, a fate god who refused their own existence.

These are but a few that you distilled into dark bottles, but we hope you remember them, remember them all. We do. Their names are written down, in the margins and back covers, on slips of cloth tied to branches, as seeming gibberish of Sacred Graffiti or hidden in the Murals along the stonework of The Fountain.

Some of those seeking the Alters in the Temple needed them, the words sometimes failing them, the Things Between sometimes unrecognizable. Your works gave them a road map, a direction, a glimmer that began in the corner of their eye for them to follow. Your works were good.

But there is always slag. Ask the bell casters of the Foundry District. Slivers of iron and cooling drops of brass on the floor, they are swept up or scraped away, but they go somewhere. The bones and scraps of grizzle, they always go somewhere. Even when recycled, the waste retains as an aspect of the Discarded. Were you not aware of this?

What else were we to do with the unexamined possibilities, unspoken words and unexpressed intentions of your rituals? They appeared here, too. Ethereal at first, in the Temple, unattached and formless next to the Alters.

And then the smoke from the apothecaries.

And then the energies released by the soothsayers.

And then the bloody bandages thrown out by the medics.

We had to build something to contain it all.

Perhaps you wanted a Queen after all. Perhaps you merely failed to recognize all of the intentions and possibilities and words of your rituals.

Now that she is gone, can you finally believe in her?

-Emelea, Steward

♦

Artisans of Foundry Alley

> *Before the revolution, you came to us and
> asked about the Bone People.*

> *We told you they were of the Between.
> We told you to trust the Queen.*

> *You maintained your worry and asked us to
> make them go away. In your love of color and
> music you found fear in their silence and in
> their pale faces.*

> *Do you remember this? Shall we say more?*

> *We told you we could not make them go away.
> Though we did not understand their true
> Nature, we knew they were somehow Of the
> City.*
> *You left, unsatisfied. And your fear of their
> silence and of their pale faces found anger
> toward us.*

> *Do you remember this? Shall we say more?*

> *You returned to Foundry Alley. You met. You
> counseled among yourselves. Without
> understanding, you conceived a plan. With
> conceit of skill, you enacted your plan. You
> selected the best artisan of each craft to
> contribute.*

> *Do you remember this? Shall we say more?*

With wood and clay and iron did you create a vessel. With subtle application did you varigate it.

Do you remember this? Shall we say more?

Then you made a bell. The most beautiful and resounding bell ever created. It never stopped ringing. Untouched, it rang on and on. The entire city could hear it. We were all enthralled. It was beautiful and unyielding. It rang out for days. Then suddenly it stopped. Without the beauty of the bell's sound, the entire city was thrown into despair. We came to you, begging to know what had happened to this greatest of all bells. In your silence, you looked guilty. But of what?

You came to us no more. Of the Bone People you asked no more. You seemed to accept their disappearance.

Do you remember this? Shall we say more?

Years later, a young apprentice, wandering the Alley, came across a shop. Inside this shop, in a darkened corner and covered in dust, this apprentice found a box. A box of wood and of iron and of clay. It felt hollow, yet it had no hinge. The apprentice returned to the temple. We looked between, as is our gift.

We saw the bell, still ringing but unheard, contained inside the box. The yearning to hear the bell was overwhelming, even after all that time.

But the bell was not all we saw.

We saw one of the Bone People. Trapped in between the walls of this vessel, of this trap you had crafted to imprison them.

Do you remember this? Shall we say more?

Already between, and being silent, and being pale, your prison drove it insane, and we were unable to release it. Yet.

-Emelea, Steward

♦

To the Masters and Guides,
To the Sages, Novices, and Tutors,
To the Teachers, Students, and the Curious,
To the Mythmakers of the Lyceum,

> *We needed to understand what we had built when we built the City.*
>
> *We had to take it apart to understand it. We needed these mythologies, and you taught them to us. Written by the wisest of you, compiled by your assistants, it was the next day that began the Age of Queens.*
>
> *Now that it is over, now that they are no longer illegal to even mention, we teach them back to you.*

Mythologies of the Age of Queens

Once upon a time, there had been a queen. A terrifying, cruel queen. The City reminds itself of this—of what the ancestors of the inhabitants fought to overthrow—each year at the Spectacle of Bells, but even those stories are mostly lost. No two tales of the Age of Queens are alike. We ask ourselves, can anyone know?

Once upon a time, there was a Queen. She was a cruel and terrible Queen. The entire population of the city was enslaved, save for a few noble families. In the Floating City, there were no prisons because the Queen would eat anyone who broke the law.

Once upon a time, there was a Queen. She never wanted to be a Queen. She wanted to be a tapestry weaver. She wanted to make music boxes. One day, she came across a milliner who tricked her into trying on a beautiful golden circlet with opals dangling from it. When it was placed on her head, she was unable to remove it. The milliner was one of the Five Devils, and said to the woman, "Now you must be Queen; you have no choice." The woman believed the devil and became Queen.

Once upon a time, there was a Queen who no one would marry because she was ugly.

Once upon a time, there was a Queen whose suitors went to war over her and claimed it was for her beauty, but really they wanted the vast wealth the City was said to have.

The Queen descended from one of the three moons.

The Queen had five children, one for each Devil.

The Queen was barren.

The Queen was a Satyress.

The Queen kept slaves but was kind to her family.

The Queen starved herself to death because she was sad.

The Queen was so beautiful that it was impossible to look upon her without weeping.

The Queen was dragged from her home by the people who lived in the City, taken to the Bazaar, and beheaded there. The slaves ate her body.

The Queen set fire to the palace one day and left, barefoot, naked, never to be seen again.

-Emelea, Steward

♦

To the Clockmakers,

You, above all others, are with the least fault. Engaged in the creation of beasts, just as often in imitation of nature as inspiration for nature, your mechanistics thrived.
It was this innocence, this naivete, that we harnessed when we asked for five clockwork mechanisms, all without a voice or heart, empty except for the mechanisms to move Her limbs and her lips. You looked curious at our request, but you built them, for us, just the same.
You see, we had a mythology, so Her heart would know our duty to serve Her.

You see, we had a vessel containing a never-ending bell, so Her voice was as beautiful as it was unendingly terrible.

You see, we had so many unspoken words and desires, so many discarded bandages, so may unrecognized intentions that they were endangering the City. None of its inhabitants understood anymore how it all worked.

You see, our Temple was overflowing, and we could no longer, in good consciousness, cast these things over the side, down onto the Lost Continent. Who knows what damage we caused. We needed a place to put them all.

You see, we made your creations live, in succession, for an Age.

You see, we were all enthralled at the sound of Her voice made by that unending bell, we reminded us all what the City was. But you already knew, didn't you? Your only blame being you were too engrossed in your creations that you never taught the rest of us.

Now the bell is broken.

For all that, we are truly, so deeply, sorry.

-Emelea, Steward

CONTRIBUTORS:

Lane Ellen

Rose Montclaire

The Clown

Ridire Quinn

Heidi Erickson

Nina Maybe

Paige Wilson

Artwork

TEEF by Elledritch Owls

Spectacle of Bells by The Maimed Typesetter

Cover Art by Todd Gnacinski\

Generous Thanks to our Beloved Editor

Sam Deges

www.ingramcontent.com/pod-product-compliance
Lightning Source LLC
Chambersburg PA
CBHW050156110726
47898CB00008B/2818